Reprint Publishing

FOR PEOPLE WHO GO FOR ORIGINALS.

I0691456

www.reprintpublishing.com

[See page 54

THE WISH BROUGHT ABOUT THE MOST ASTONISHING
RESULTS

Jack and the Check Book

By
John
Kendrick
Bangs

Illustrated
by
Albert
Levering

HARPER & BROTHERS
NEW YORK and LONDON
19   11

COPYRIGHT, 1911, BY HARPER & BROTHERS
PRINTED IN THE UNITED STATES OF AMERICA
PUBLISHED MAY, 1911

CONTENTS

ILLUSTRATIONS

ILLUSTRATIONS

JACK AND THE CHECK-BOOK

JACK AND
THE CHECK-BOOK

I

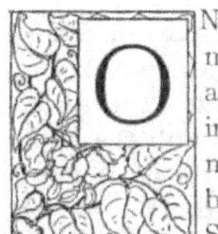NCE upon a time a great many years ago there lived a poor woman who, having invested all her savings in mining shares, was soon brought to penury and want. She had bought her modest little home and all there was in it on the instalment plan, and here she was, upon a certain beautiful morning in late spring, absolutely penniless, and three days off, staring her in the face, were payments due on the piano, the kitchen range and even

on the house itself. Moreover, the winter had been a bitter one. Four times had the water - pipes frozen and burst, and a plumber's bill of appalling magnitude had come in the morning's mail, with the stern admonition stamped in red letters at the bottom:

LONG PAST DUE.
PLEASE REMIT.

The unhappy woman was at her wit's ends to know what to do. She had tried to sell her shares in "Amalgamated War-whoop," only to find that that once prom-ising company had passed into the hands of a receiver, and that there was an assess-ment, amounting to four times their face value, due on the shares, so that every pos-sible purchaser to whom she applied re-fused to take the stock off her hands unless she paid them five dollars a share for the service and would guarantee them against the chance of further loss. All other means of raising the necessary funds—and she had tried them all—proved equally futile. The savings-banks would not lend her a penny on a house of which the parlor floor alone was clear of obligation, and the threat of the piano people to remove that instrument if the March instalment, now a month overdue, was not immediately forthcoming rendered that both unsalable and valueless as security for a loan.

She sat, the perfect picture of hopeless despair, in her rocking-chair, gazing moodily out of the window, thinking dreadful thoughts, and, it may be, contemplating the alternative of suicide or marriage with the village magnate, a miserable villain whom everybody detested, and who, everybody knew very well, had been instrumental in the ruin of her deceased husband, a once prosperous haberdasher. But on a sudden her look of despair faded wholly away and a great light of happiness illumined her eyes, as up the garden path, whistling merrily as he strode along, came her son

JACK AND THE CHECK-BOOK

Jack, a lad of fifteen, the comfort and solace of her lonely days.

"Dear boy!" she murmured softly to herself as he waved his hand at her, "he is the only thing I have left that there isn't something due on."

The boy, entering the room, still whistling, flung his cap up on the table and kissed his mother affectionately.

"Well, mother," he said, joyously, "our troubles are over at last."

Her face beamed an eager inquiry. The sudden, overwhelming happiness of the news itself deprived her of the power of speech for a moment, and then with difficulty she gasped out the words:

"Then you have

4

secured a place with steady wages, my son?"

Her heart beat wildly as she awaited the answer.

"No, mother," he replied, promptly. "The only position open to me was that of private secretary to old Jonas Bilkins, my father's enemy, and when he found out that I was my father's son he fired me out of his office."

"No wonder!" muttered the woman. "He didn't dare let you have access to his private papers. He knows that every penny he calls his own belongs by right to us, and once you got hold of his letter-files and secret documents you could prove it."

5

"So he said, mother dear," said the boy. "He was brutally frank about it, and when I told him what I thought of him, and advised him to pick out a nice, comfortable jail to spend his declining years in, he threw his check-book at my head."

"The miserable villain!" groaned the old lady. "Did it hit you?"

"No, indeed," laughed Jack. "My baseball training helped me out there. I caught it on the fly and have brought it home with me. Meanwhile, I have sold the cow."

"You have?" cried the delighted mother, clasping him warmly in her arms.

"Yes," said Jack, proudly. "We need not go hungry to-day, mother. I swapped her off for a pot of beans."

An awful, despairing silence followed this announcement. The old lady loved her son beyond everything in the world, but this was too much even for a mother's love. The idea that a first-class Jersey cow worth not less than forty-five dollars regarded

THE BEANS SCATTERED IN EVERY DIRECTION

merely as raw material for the table, and not taking into account her value as a producer of rich, creamy milk, should have been bartered for a miserable pot of beans, and doubtless pickled beans at that, was the last straw of misfortune that broke the back of the Camel of Maternal Patience, and with certain phrases of a forceful nature she seized the pot from her son's trembling hand and flung it with such impetus against the garden wall that it was shattered into countless fragments, and the beans scattered in every direction. After this attack of rage she took to her bed, weeping bitterly. Jack too, stunned by his kind mother's wrath, retired to his little cot in the attic, and sought relief from his troubles and the gnawing pangs of hunger in sleep.

But lo and behold! the following morning a strange thing had happened. Jack, upon waking early, found his once sunny window obscured by a heavy growth of leaves, and on dressing rapidly and going into the gar-

9

den to see what had caused this strange condition of affairs, was surprised to find a splendid bean-stalk sprung up during the night, and, what was still more wonderful, still springing, moving rapidly upward like the escalator he had once seen upon the elevated railway in New York when with his father he had visited that wonderful city to inspect the spring and autumn styles for the haberdashery.

He gazed at it in wondering amazement, and then the silence was broken. "All aboard for Ogreville!" cried a squeaky little voice from behind one of the branches. "Step lively, please! All aboard!"

Jack, nothing loath for a new experience, immediately seated himself astride one of the rapidly rising tendrils, and soon found himself soaring in the upper air, far, far above the earth, upon what he came subsequently to call his " Aero-Bean."

"Well, we have you at last," said the squeaky little voice from behind the leaves, pleasantly. "You may not remember it, my lad, but you once gave up your strap on a subway train to a tired-looking woman and she has never forgotten your kindness. It so happens that she was Queen of the Fairies, and later on she became Chairman of the Board of Directors of the United States Fairy Corporation of Wall Street. You are now about to receive your reward. You have Major Bilkins's check-book with you?"

"Yes," said Jack. "He threw it at me yesterday, and I've had it ever since."

"Good!" said the squeaky little voice. "What is the old man's balance?"

"Three million five hundred and seventy-five thousand four hundred and fifty-seven dollars," said Jack, reading off the figures slowly, and gasping at the thought of any-body's having so much money as that on hand.

"H'm!" said the squeaky little voice. "It is rather less than I had thought.

However, we can fix that without much trouble. Zeros are cheap. Just add six of them to that balance."

"Do you mean add or affix?" asked Jack.

"Affix is what I should have said," replied the squeaky little voice. "Get out your fountain pen and tag 'em on."

Jack immediately obeyed.

"Now what does it come to?" asked the little voice.

"Three trillion five hundred and seventy-five billion four hundred and fifty-seven million dollars," stammered Jack, his eyes bulging with amazement.

"That's better," laughed the little voice. "Thus you see, my boy, how easy it is to make much out of a little if you only know how. Three and a half trillions is a pretty tidy bit of pocket-money for a boy of your age. So be careful how you use it, my son. Use it wisely, and all will be well with you."

As the voice spoke these words the grow-

ing stalk came to a sudden stop, and the
voice added:

"Ogreville! Last stop! All out!"

The boy stepped off the stalk, and found
himself in a magnificently broad and fertile
country. Great fields of waving grain, num-
berless pasturages filled with prize cattle of
all sorts, surrounded him on every hand.
Trees heavily laden with rare fruits bordered
the highways, and everything everywhere
bore unmistakable evidences of a rare prosperity.

"Phe-e-ew!" whistled Jack, blinking with
joy at all he saw before him. "This looks
like the land of milk and honey all right.
And only twenty minutes by bean-car from
New York! What a chance for corner lots,
and an easy suburb for business men!"

The lad wandered along for a while, re-
joicing in all the beauties of the wondrous
scene, when, coming to a turn in the magnificently laid road, he perceived not far ahead
of him a splendidly built castle, much re-

13

sembling a famous city hotel he had once passed on a sight-seeing coach, and, remembering on a sudden that he had had no breakfast, he walked boldly up to the main entrance and knocked on the massive bronze door. A beautiful young girl about his own age answered the summons.

"I don't know if this is a hotel," said Jack, politely, "but if it is, might I get a bite here?"

"I fear you might if my stepfather should happen to see you," replied the girl with a shudder, her face mantling with a deep luscious red, the like of which Jack had never seen anywhere save on the petal of a rose or the cheek of a cherry.

The silvery tones of her voice thrilled him.

"Thank you," he said, stepping into the hallway through the open door. "I shall be very glad to meet your stepfather, and if, while I am waiting, I might have a couple of scrambled eggs and a cup of coffee—"

"Oh, go! Do not stay here!" pleaded the girl. "Please go!"

"I go?" laughed Jack. "And leave you? Never!"

"But you do not understand," trembled the girl. "My stepfather is an ogre, and he eats—"

"I only understand one thing," said Jack, valiantly. "And that is that I love you with all my heart. I don't care if your stepfather eats—"

"For my sake then, go!" pleaded the girl. "I too am not unsusceptible to the dart of love, and for the first time I look upon a spirit I could honor and obey, but—"

"Then it is love at first sight for both of us," said Jack, folding her in his arms.

It was indeed a blissful moment for both, but alas! it was more than fleeting, for suddenly there came from an inner room off the great corridor a terrific voice, roaring:

"FEE-FO-FI-FOY!
I SMELL THE BLOOD OF A HIGH-SCHOOL BOY.
BE HE REAL OR BE HE FAKE
I'LL GRIND HIS BONES FOR A BUCKWHEAT
CAKE."

"Oho!" cried Jack, springing back. "I think I've heard something like that before. This is not a hotel, but the castle of that child-eating ogre—"

"The very same!" cried the girl, her face blanching with terror. "And, what is worse, he hasn't had a boy to eat for three weeks. If you truly love me, I beg you will fly at once."

"Sorry to be disobliging, but I can't fly, my beloved. I've left my aeroplane at home. In short, my dear-er-er—what is your name, sweetheart?"

"Beanhilda," replied the blushing girl.

"In short, my dear Beanhilda," Jack resumed, "having no wings, I cannot fly."

"Alas!" cried the girl, bursting into floods

of tears as the ogre suddenly appeared in the hallway, and seizing Jack by the collar of his coat held him high in the air between his thumb and forefinger. "Alas! it is too late. I shall never get a fiancé past step-papa's breakfast-table!"

"No, my child," grinned the ogre, smacking his lips hungrily. "It is not too late. He is just in time. I have been wanting a couple of poached boys on toast for three solid weeks, and the butcher has just telephoned me that there isn't a fresh kid to be had for love or money in any of the markets."

"I am sorry to disappoint you, Mr. Ogre," said Jack, as calmly as he could under the trying circumstances, "but I won't poach well. I'm half-back on our high-school eleven, and, as a matter of fact, am known as the toughest lad in my native town."

A shadow of disappointment crossed the ogre's face.

"Confound football!" he growled. "I

haven't managed to get a tender boy since the season opened."

"Moreover," said Jack, seeing that the time for strategy had arrived, "I didn't come here for your breakfast, I came for mine."

"By Jove, you shall have it!" cried the ogre, slapping the table with his fists so hard that the platters and glasses upon its broad surface jumped up and down. "I like nerve, and you are the only kid I've caught in forty years that didn't begin to yell like mad the minute I grabbed him. We'll keep you here and feed you on the fat of the land, until you have sort of softened up. Sit down, sir, and have your fill. Beanhilda, get the lad a cup of coffee."

The ogre placed Jack in a high-chair at his side, and they breakfasted together like two old cronies, the fair Beanhilda waiting upon them, and with every passing moment convincing Jack, by her grace, beauty, and amiability, of the solid fact that he loved her

18

ardently. It was a terrible sight to see the ogre swallow a whole lamb at one bite, taking it up by its tail and dropping it into his mouth as if it were no more than a stalk of asparagus, and consuming not less than fifty-seven varieties of breakfast food, boxes, wrapping, premiums and all at one spoonful, but the lad's nerve never deserted him for a moment, and he chatted away as pleasantly as though breakfasting with ogres was one of the accustomed operations of his every-day life.

"This is a great place you have here, Mr. Ogre," he remarked, sipping his coffee slowly. "Of course, it isn't quite as rich and fertile as my own little place up in Vermont, and your cattle, though evidently of fine breed, are hardly what Montana ranchmen would consider first class. Still—"

The ogre stopped eating and looked at the speaker with considerable surprise.

"You mean to say you can beat this place of mine anywhere?" he demanded.

"Well," said Jack, amiably, "of course I don't mean to criticise this beautiful country. It is very beautiful in its own way, and there is some evidence of wealth here. I was only saying that next to my place it comes pretty near to being the finest I ever saw."

"I guess you'd go a good many miles before you'd see a castle like mine," said the ogre, with a proud glance around him.

"I haven't seen your castle yet, sir," said Jack. "But this little bungalow we are in strikes me as about as cute and comfy a cozy-corner as I've visited in a month of Sundays."

"Bungalow?" roared the giant. "You don't call this a bungalow, do you?"

"Why, yes," said Jack. "It certainly isn't a tent, or a chicken-coop, or a tool-house, is it? It's mighty comfy anyhow, whatever you call it. I wouldn't mind owning it myself."

A glitter came into the ogre's eyes. If

this young man were merely bluffing now was the time to call him.

"Oh; as for that," said the ogre, with a sarcastic laugh, "you can own it—that is, you can if you can pay for it. I'll sell."

Here he winked at the butler as much as to say, "Now we'll see him flop." But Jack had no intention of flopping.

"Really?" he said, with a great show of enthusiasm. "Well, this is fine. I hadn't the slightest idea the place was in the market, but if we can get together on a figure, I might be tempted. How much?"

"What would you say to $2,500,000?" demanded the ogre, with a grim smile.

"Done!" said Jack. "And cheap at the price."

Here he drew out the check-book, and drew a check for the full amount to the order of William J. Ogre, Esq., which he tossed across the table to the amazed giant.

"There's your money," he said. "Fork over the deeds."

The ogre rubbed his eyes, and almost stopped breathing for a moment.

"H'm!" he muttered, inspecting the check closely. "This looks pretty good to me. What kind of a book is that, young man?"

"That?" laughed Jack. "Oh, that's what we call the magic check-book. It is the kind that all our big financiers use—Mr. Rockernegie, Colonel Midas, and John Jacob Rothschild, and all the rest of them. It is merely an ingenious financial contrivance that enables us to avoid contact with actual money, which is not only vulgar and dangerous to carry in large quantities, but in some cases is full of germs." The lad went on and explained to the ogre just how checks were drawn and presented for payment.

"It's a pretty nice sort of an arrangement, that," said the ogre, very much interested, "but suppose you draw out your whole balance, what then?"

"All you have to do is to affix a half dozen ciphers to the remainder before you start

THE OGRE COLLAPSED IN HIS CHAIR

the overdraft," said Jack. "For instance, on my way up here this morning I found that the balance on hand was only $3,-575,457, so, feeling that I should be more comfortable with just a little more ready money to carry me along, I added those six ciphers you see on the right-hand side of the figures, bringing the balance up to $3,575,457,000,000. If you will examine the ciphers under a microscope, sir, you will note that they have only recently been entered."

"By thunder!" roared the ogre, glaring at the book enviously. "This is one of the marvels of the age. Why, armed with a book like that you can buy anything in sight!"

"If the other man will sell," said Jack. "By-the-way, would you mind if I lit my after-breakfast cigarette?"

"Go ahead! Go ahead! Do anything you darn please," said the ogre, gazing at him with wonder.

Jack thereupon drew a check for $500,000,

tore it from the book, and rolled it into a small cylinder, which he filled with some corn-silk he had in his pocket, and then lit it with another check for a similar amount.

The ogre's eyes nearly popped out of his head at such a marvellous exhibition of resources.

"It makes an expensive smoke," smiled Jack, settling back to the enjoyment of the cigarette, "but after all, as long as I have the money, why not enjoy myself? Will you join me?"

He took up his pen as though to make another.

"No, no, no!" cried the ogre, walking agitatedly up and down the floor. "I—er —I'm afraid it's too soon after breakfast for me. Do you mean to tell me that such an inexhaustible treasure as this really exists?"

"There it is, right before your eyes," said Jack. "Suppose we test it. Think of a large sum of money, tell me what it is, and see if I can't go you a dollar better."

"BLESS YOU, MY CHILDREN!"

"Four hundred millions!" cried the ogre, impulsively.

"Piker!" ejaculated Jack, with a smile, as he drew his check for $400,000,001.

"A billion and a half!" cried the ogre.

"Now you're beginning to get your pace," laughed Jack. "There's my check, sir, for $1,500,000,001, according to specifications."

"That reduces your balance some, though," said the ogre.

"Yes," said Jack. "It reduces it by $1,900,000,002, leaving me with only $3,-573,574,999,998 on hand, but if I affix six ciphers to that, as I will now proceed to do, I have, as the figures conclusively show, $3,575,574,999,998,000,000, or about a squillion more than I had before I began to draw."

The ogre collapsed in his chair. The magnitude of these figures appalled him.

"Great glory!" he cried. "I didn't know there was that much money in the world. Can—can anybody work that book?"

"Anybody who comes by it honestly and without trickery," said Jack. "Of course, if a man gets hold of it in an unscrupulous way, or goes back on his bargain, it's as valueless to him as so much waste paper."

The ogre strode up and down the room, filled with agitation. He had thought to trick the boy out of his wonderful possession —in fact, to swallow him whole and then appropriate his treasure, but Jack's explanation put an entirely new phase on the matter.

"I suppose you wouldn't part with that book?" he finally asked.

"Yes," said Jack. "I'll let you have it if you will transfer all your property irrevocably to your stepdaughter, Beanhilda, and give me her hand in marriage."

"It's a bargain!" gulped the ogre, whereupon he summoned his lawyers and his secretaries, and by noon all his possessions had passed beyond recall into the hands of Beanhilda. A special messenger was sent

"A WEEK'S VACATION IN LITTLE OLD NEW YORK"

down the bean-stalk to fetch Jack's mother, and that afternoon the happy lad and the fair Princess of Ogreville were married with much pomp and ceremony.

"Bless you, my children!" murmured the ogre, as the irrevocable words were spoken by the priest, and Jack passed the magic check-book over to its new owner. "May you live long and happily. As for me, I'm off for a week's vacation in little old New York."

"How did you manage it, sweetheart?" whispered Beanhilda in her husband's ear a few weeks later. "Step-papa had such a penchant for hard-boiled boys that I feared you were lost the moment he appeared."

Jack explained the whole history of the magic check-book to her, but when he had done, his bride grew white.

"But what if he comes back?" she cried, shuddering with fear. "His vengeance will be terrible."

JACK AND THE CHECK-BOOK

"Have no fear, Beanhilda," Jack answered. "He will not return. Read that."

And he handed her an evening paper in which, with rapidly drying eyes, she read the following:

SEVENTY-FIVE YEARS FOR PASSING BAD CHECKS

William J. Ogre, claiming to be a prominent resident of Ogreville, who was arrested at the St. Gotham Hotel last Thursday afternoon on a charge of having passed a dozen bogus checks for amounts ranging from ten to fifteen thousand dollars apiece, was found guilty yesterday by a jury in the criminal branch of the United States Circuit Court. He was sentenced to fifteen years' imprisonment at hard labor in the Federal Prison at Thomasville, Georgia, on each of the five different counts, making his prison term in all not less than seventy-five years. Other indictments are still pending against him for forgery on the complaint of Major Bilkins, president of the Suburban Trust Company, of whose name he was found availing himself in his criminal transactions. Major Bilkins, when seen last night by a reporter of this paper, stated his intention of keeping the shameless operator in jail for the rest of his natural life.

JACK AND THE CHECK-BOOK

"I shouldn't sit up for papa if I were you, Beanhilda," said Jack, with a smile. "It looks to me as if he was going to be detained down-town late on business."

And the young couple lived happily forever after.

II

THE GREAT WISH SYNDICATE

T HE farm had gone to ruin. On every side the pastures were filled with a rank growth of thistles and other thorn - bearing flora. The farm buildings had fallen into a condition of hopeless disrepair, and the old house, the ancestral home of the Wilbrahams, had become a place of appalling desolation. The roof had been patched and repatched for decades, and now fulfilled none of the ideals of its roof-hood save that of antiquity. There was not, as far as the eye could see, a single whole pane of glass in any one of the many windows of the mansion, and there were not wanting those in the community who were willing to prophesy that in a stiff gale—such as used to be prevalent in that section of the world, and within the recollection of some of the old settlers too—the chimneys, once the pride of the county, would totter and fall, bringing the whole mansion down into chaos and ruin. In short, the one-time model farm of the Wilbrahams had become a by-word and a jest and, as some said, of no earthly use save for the particular purposes of the eccentric artist in search of picturesque subject-matter for his studies in oil.

It was a wild night, and within the ancient house sat the owner, Richard Wilbraham, his wife not far away, trying to find room upon her husband's last remaining pair of socks to darn them. Wilbraham gazed silently into the glowing embers on the hearth before them, the stillness of the evening broken only by the hissing of the logs on the andirons and an occasional sigh from one of the watchers.

Finally the woman spoke.

"When does the mortgage fall due, Richard?" she asked, moving uneasily in her chair.

"To-morrow," gulped the man, the word seeming to catch in his throat and choke him.

"And you—you are sure Colonel Digby will not renew it?" she queried.

"He even declines to discuss the matter," said Wilbraham. "He contents himself with shaking it in my face every time I approach his office, while he tells his office-boy to escort me to the door. I don't believe in signs, Ethelinda, but I do believe that that is an omen that if the money is not forthcoming at noon to-morrow you and I will be roofless by this time to-morrow night."

The woman shuddered.

"But, Richard," she protested, "you—

WITHIN THE ANCIENT HOUSE SAT THE OWNER, RICHARD WILBRAHAM

you had put by the money to pay it long ago. What has become of it?"

"Gone, Ethelinda—gone in that ill-advised egg deal I tried to put through two years ago," sighed Wilbraham, as he buried his face in his hands to hide his grief and mortification. "I sold eggs short," he added. "You remember when that first batch of incubator hens began laying so prolifically—it seemed to me as though Fortune stared me in the face—nay, held out her hands to me and bade me welcome to a share in her vast estates. There was a great shortage of eggs in the market that year, and I went to New York and sold them by the dozens—hundreds of dozens—thousands of dozens—"

He rose up from his chair and paced the floor in an ecstasy of agitation. "I sold eggs by the million, Ethelinda," he went on, by a great effort regaining control of himself. "Eggs to be laid by hens whose great-great-great-grandmothers had yet to be hatched from eggs yet unlaid by unborn chickens."

Wilbraham's voice sank to a hoarse, guttural whisper.

"And the deliveries have bankrupted me," he muttered. "The price of eggs has risen steadily for the past eighteen months, and yesterday a hundred thousand of January, strictly fresh, that I had to buy in the open market in order to fill my contracts, cost me not only my last penny, but were in part paid for with a sixty-day note that I cannot hope to meet. In other words, Ethelinda, we are ruined."

The woman made a brave struggle to be strong, but the strain was too much for her tired nerves and she broke down and wept bitterly.

"We have but four hens left," Wilbraham went on, speaking in a hollow voice. "At most, working them to their full capacity, in thirty days from now we shall have only ten dozen eggs added to our present store, and upon that date I have promised to deliver to the International Cold Storage Company one thousand dozen at twenty-two and a half cents a dozen. Even with the mortgage out of the way we should still be securely bound in the clutch of bankruptcy."

A long silence ensued. The clock out in the hall ticked loudly, each clicking sound falling upon Wilbraham's ears like a sledge-hammer blow in a forge, welding link by link a chain of ruin that should forever bind him in the shackles of misery. Unbroken save by the banging now and then of a shutter in the howling wind without, the silence continued for nearly an hour, when the nerve-killing monotony of the ceaseless "tick-tock, tick-tock" of the clock was varied by a resounding hammering upon the door.

"It is very late," said the woman. "Who do you suppose can be calling at this hour? Be careful when you open the door—it may be a highwayman."

"I should welcome a highwayman if he could help me to find anything in the house worth stealing," said Wilbraham, as he rose from his chair and started for the door. "Whoever it may be, it is a wild night, and despite our poverty we can still keep open house for the stranger on the moor."

He hastened to the door and flung it wide.

"Who's there?" he cried, gazing out into the blackness of the storm.

A heavy gust of wind, icy cold, blew out his candle, and a great mass of sleet coming in with it fell with a dull, sodden thud on the floor at his feet, and some of it cut his cheek.

"I am a wanderer," came a faint voice from without, "frozen and starved. In the name of humanity I beg you to take me in, lest I faint and perish."

"Come in, come in!" cried Wilbraham. "Whoever you are, you are more than welcome to that which is left us; little enough in all conscience."

An aged man, bent and weary, staggered

44

in through the door. Wilbraham sprang
toward him and caught his fainting form in
his strong arms. Tenderly he led him to
his own abandoned chair by the fireside,
where he and his faithful wife chafed the old
fellow's hands until warmth had returned to
them.

"A cup of tea, my dear," said Wilbraham.
"It will set him up."

"And a morsel to eat, I implore you,"
pleaded the stranger, in a weak, tremulous
voice. "The merest trifle, good sir, even if
it be only an egg!"

The woman grew rigid at the suggestion.
"An egg? At this time when eggs are—"
she began.

"There, there, Ethelinda," interrupted
Wilbraham, gently. "We have two left in
the ice-box—your breakfast and mine.
Rather than see this good old man suffer
longer I will gladly go without mine. The
fact is, eggs have sort of disagreed with me
latterly anyhow, and—"

45

"It is as you say, Richard," said the woman, meekly, as with a hopeless sigh she turned toward the kitchen, whence in a short time she returned, bearing a steaming creation of her own make—a lustrous, golden egg, poached, and lying invitingly upon the crisp bosom of a piece of toast. It was a sight of beauty, and Wilbraham's mouth watered as he gazed hungrily upon it.

And then the unexpected happened: The aged stranger, instead of voraciously devouring the proffered meal, with a kindly glance upon his host, raised his withered hands aloft as though to pronounce a benediction upon him, and in a chanting tone droned forth the lines:

"Who eats this egg and toast delicious
Receives the gift of three full wishes—
Thus do the fairy folk reward
The sacrifices of this board."

A low, rumbling peal of thunder and a blinding flash as of the lightning followed, and when the brilliant illumination of the latter had died away the stranger had vanished.

Wilbraham looked at his wife, dumb with amazement, and she, tottering backward into her chair, gazed back, her eyes distended with fear.

"Have I—have I been dreaming?" he gasped, recovering his speech in a moment. "Or have we really had a visitor?"

"I was going to ask you the same question, Richard," she replied. "It really was so very extraordinary, I can hardly believe—"

And then their eyes fell upon the steaming egg, still lying like a beautiful sunset on a background of toast upon the table.

"The egg!" she cried, hoarsely. "It must have been true."

"Will you eat it?" asked Wilbraham, politely extending the platter in her direction.

"Never!" she cried, shuddering. "I should not dare. It is too uncanny."

"Then I will," said Wilbraham. "If the old man spoke the truth—"

He swallowed the egg at a single gulp.

"Fine!" he murmured, in an ecstasy of gastronomic pleasure. "I wish there were two more just like it!"

No sooner had he spoken these words than two more poached eggs, even as he had wished, appeared upon the platter.

"Great heavens, Ethelinda!" he cried. "The wishes come true! I wish to goodness I knew who that old duffer was."

The words had scarcely fallen from his lips when a card fluttered down from the ceiling. Wilbraham sprang forward excitedly and caught it as it fell. It read:

HENRY W. OBERON

Secretary, The United States Fairy Co.,

3007 Wall Street

"Henry W. Oberon, United States Fairy Company, Wall Street, eh?" he muttered. "By Jove, I wish I knew—"

"Stop!" cried his wife, seizing him by the arm, imploringly. "Do stop, Richard. You have used up two of your wishes already. Think what you need most before you waste the third."

"Wise Ethelinda," he murmured, patting her gently on the hand. "Very, very wise, and I will be careful. Let me see now. . . . I wish I had . . . I wish I had . . ."

He paused for a long time, and then his face fairly beamed with a great light of joy.

"I wish I had three more wishes!" he cried.

Another crash of thunder shook the house to its very foundations, and a lightning flash turned the darkness of the interior of the dwelling into a vivid golden yellow that dazzled them, and then all went dusk again.

"Mercy!" shuddered the good wife. "I hope that was an answer to your wish."

"It won't take long to find out," said Wilbraham. "I'll tackle a few more natural desires right here and now, and if they come true I'll know that that thunderbolt was a rush message from the United States Fairy Company telling me to draw on them at sight."

"Well, don't be extravagant," his wife cautioned him.

"I'll be as extravagant as I please," he retorted. "If my fourth wish works, Ethelinda, my address from this hour on will be Easy Street and Treasury Avenue. I wish first then that this old farm was in Ballyhack!"

"Ballyhack! Last station — all out!" cried a hoarse voice at the door.

Wilbraham rushed to the window and peered out into what had been the night, but had now become a picture of something worse. Great clouds of impenetrable smoke hung over the grim stretches of a dismal-looking country in which there seemed to be nothing but charred remnants of ruined trees and blackened rocks, over which, in an endless line, a weary mass of struggling plodders,

"BALLYHACK! LAST STATION—ALL OUT!"

men and women, toiled onward through the grime of a hopeless environment.

"Great Scott!" he cried, in dismay, as the squalid misery of the prospect smote upon his vision. "This is worse than Diggville. I wish to heaven we were back again."

"Diggville! Change cars for Easy Street and Fortune Square!" cried the hoarse voice at the door, and Wilbraham, looking out through the window again, was rejoiced to find himself back amid familiar scenes.

"They're working all right," he said, gleefully.

"Yes," said his wife. "They seem to be and you seem to be speculating as usual upon a narrow margin. Again you have only one wish left, having squandered four out of the five already used."

"And why not, my dear," smiled Wilbraham, amiably, "when my next wish is to be for six spandy new wishes straight from the factory?"

Mrs. Wilbraham's face cleared.

"Oh, splendid!" she cried, joyously. "Wish it—wish it—do hurry before you forget."

"I do wish it—six more wishes on the half-shell!" roared Wilbraham.

As before, came the thunder and the lightning.

"Thank you!" said Wilbraham. "These fairies are mighty prompt correspondents. I am beginning to see my way out of our difficulties, Ethelinda," he proceeded, rubbing his hands together unctuously. "Instead of dreading to-morrow and the maturity of that beastly old mortgage, I wish to thunder it were here, and that the confounded thing were paid off."

The wish, expressed impulsively, brought about the most astonishing results. The hall clock began instantly to whirr and to wheeze, its hands whizzing about as though upon a well-oiled pivot. The sun shot up out of the eastern horizon as though fired from a cannon, and before the amazed

54

couple could realize what was going on, the
village clock struck the hour of noon, and
they found themselves bowing old Colonel
Digby, the mortgage holder, out of the
house, while Wilbraham himself held in his
right hand a complete satisfaction of that
depressing document.

"Now," said Wilbraham, "I feel like
celebrating. What would you say to a nice
little luncheon, my dear? Something simple, but good—say some Russian caviare,
Lynnhaven Bay oysters, real turtle soup,
terrapin, canvas-back duck, alligator-pear
salad, and an orange brûlot for two, eh?"

"It would be fine, Richard," replied the
lady, her eyes flashing with joy, "but I don't
know where we could get such a feast here.
The Diggville markets are—"

"Markets?" cried Wilbraham, contemp-
tuously. "What have we to do with markets from this time on? Markets are nothing to me. I merely wish that we had that
repast right here and now, ready to—"

"Luncheon is served, sir," said a tall, majestic-looking stranger, entering from the dining-room.

"Ah! Really?" said Wilbraham. "And who the dickens are you?"

"I am the head butler of the Fairies' Union assigned to your service, sir," replied the stranger, civilly, making a low bow to Mrs. Wilbraham.

There is no use of describing the meal. It was all there as foreshadowed in Wilbraham's gastronomically inspired menu, and having had nothing to eat since the night before, the fortunate couple did full justice to it.

"Before we go any further, Richard," said Mrs. Wilbraham, after the duck had been served, "do you happen to remember how many of your last six wishes are left?"

"No, I don't," said Wilbraham.

"Then you had better order a few more lest by the end of this charming repast you forget," said the thoughtful woman.

56

"Good scheme, Ethelinda," said Wilbraham. "I'll put in a bid for a gross right away. There is no use in piking along in small orders when you can do a land-office business without lifting your little finger."

"And don't you think, too, dear," the woman continued, "that it would be well for us to open a set of books—a sort of General Wish Account—so that we shall not at any time by some unfortunate mistake overdraw our balance?"

"Ethelinda," cried Wilbraham, his face glowing with enthusiastic admiration, "you have, without any exception, the best business head that ever wore a pompadour!"

Thus it began. A cash-book was purchased and in its columns, like so many entries of mere dollars, Wilbraham entered his income in wishes, faithfully recording on the opposite page his expenditures in the same. The first entry of one gross was made that very night:

March 16, 19—, Sight Draft on U. S. Fairy Co., 144

Before long others followed and were used to such an effect that at the end of the year, by a careful manipulation of his resources, carefully husbanding the possibilities of that original third wish, Wilbraham found that he had expressed and had had gratified over ten thousand wishes, all of such a nature that the one-time decrepit farm had now become one of the handsomest estates in the country. A château stood on the site of the old mansion. Where the barns had been in danger of falling of their own weight were now to be found rows of well-stocked cattle-houses and dairies of splendor. The decaying stables had become garages of unusual magnificence, wherein cars of all horse-powers and models panted, eager to be chugging over the roads of Diggville, which by a single wish expressed by Wilbraham had become wondrously paved boulevards. And in the chicken-yards that had taken the place of the discouraging coops of other days thousands of hens laid their daily quota of prosperity for their owner in the plush-upholstered nests provided for their comfort by Wilbraham, the egg king, for that was what he had now become. In all parts of the world his fame was heralded, and hosts of sight-seers came daily to see the wonderful acres of this lordly master of the world's egg supply. And, best of all, there was still a balance of forty-three hundred and eighty-seven wishes to his credit!

The leading financiers of the world now began to take notice of this new figure in the realm of effort, for they soon found their most treasured and surest schemes going awry in a most unaccountable manner. No matter how much they tried to depress or to stimulate the market, some new and strange factor seemed to be at work bringing their calculations to naught, and when it became known to them that the mere expression of a wish on the part of Wilbraham would send stocks kiting into the air or crashing into the

59

depths, no matter what they might do, they began to worry.

"To-morrow," said John W. Midas, as he talked to Wilbraham and his friends one evening at the club, "International Gold Brick Common will fall off thirty-seven points."

"Not so, Colonel," Wilbraham had retorted. "It will rise seventy points."

"Oh, it will, will it? How do you know that?" demanded Midas.

"Because I wish it," said Wilbraham.

And on the morrow International Gold Brick, opening at 96⅝, lo and behold! closed at 166⅝, and the friends of Midas who had laughed at Wilbraham and sold short went to the wall. A half-dozen experiences of a similar nature showed the former rulers of the financial world that Wilbraham had now become a force to be reckoned with, and for their own protection the more eminent among them called a meeting at the home of Mr. Andrew Rockernegie to consider the situation. There was too much power in the hands of one man, they thought, although that idea had never occurred to any of them before. The result of the meeting was that Colonel Midas was appointed a committee of one to call upon Wilbraham and see what could be done.

"You may not be aware of it, Mr. Wilbraham," said the Colonel, "but by your occasional intrusions into our lines of work you are making finance an inexact science. Now, what will you take to keep your hands off the market altogether? Twenty millions?"

Wilbraham laughed.

"Really, Colonel Midas," he replied, "I had no idea that you ever did business on a corner-grocery basis like that. You ought to run a vacuum cleaner over your brow. I think there are cobwebs in your gray matter. Why, my dear sir, I can capitalize this gift of mine at a billion, and pay ten per cent. on every dollar of it every year, with a little melon to be cut up annually by the stockholders of one hundred and fifty per cent. per annum. Why, then, should I sell out at twenty millions?"

"Oh, I suppose you can have the earth if you want it," retorted Midas, ruefully. "But all the same—"

"No, I don't want the earth," said Wilbraham. "If I had wanted it I should have had it long ago. I'd only have to pay taxes on it, and it would be a nuisance looking after the property."

"On what basis will you sell out?" demanded Midas.

"Well, we might incorporate my gift," said Wilbraham. "What would you say to a United States Wish Syndicate, formed to produce and sell wishes to the public by the can—POTTED WISHES: ONE HUNDRED NON-CUMULATIVE WISHES FOR A DOLLAR. Eh?"

Midas paced the floor in his enthusiasm.

"Magnificent!" he cried. "We'll underwrite the whole thing in my office—bonds, stock, both common and preferred—for say—ahem!—how much did you say?"

"Oh, I guess I can pull along on a billion," said Wilbraham. "Cash."

Midas scratched his head. A glitter came into his eye.

"You wish to give up control of your gift?" he asked.

"You are a clever man, Colonel Midas," grinned Wilbraham. "If I had said 'yes' to that question I'd have lost my power. But I'm too old a bird to be caught that way. You go ahead and form your company, and sell your securities to the public at par, pay me my billion, and I'll transfer the business to you, C. O. D."

"Done!" said Midas, and he returned to his fellow-captains on the Street.

Wilbraham was felicitating himself upon a wondrously good stroke of business, when another caller entered his room, this time unannounced.

"How do you do, Mr. Wilbraham?" said the stranger, as he mysteriously materialized before Wilbraham's desk.

"How are you?" said Wilbraham. "Your face is familiar to me, but I can't just recall where I have met you."

"My name is Oberon, sir," said the stranger, "I am the secretary of the United States Fairy Company. There is a little trouble over your account, and I have called to see if we can't—"

Wilbraham's heart sank within him.

"It—it isn't overdrawn, is it?" he whispered, hoarsely.

"No, it isn't," said the secretary.

"By Jove!" cried Wilbraham, drawing a deep sigh of relief, and springing to his feet, grasping Oberon by both hands. "Sit down, sit down! You have been a benefactor to me, sir."

"I am glad you realize that fact, Mr. Wilbraham," said the fairy, somewhat coldly. "It makes it easier for me to say

64

what I have come here to say. We did not
realize, Mr. Wilbraham," he went on, "when
we awarded you the three original wishes
that you would be clever enough to work the
wish business up into an industry. If we
had we should have made the wishes non-
cumulative. We were perfectly willing to
permit a reasonable overdraft also, but we
didn't expect you to pyramid your holdings
the way you have done until you have practically secured a corner in the market."

Wilbraham grinned broadly.

"I have been going some," he said.

"Rather," said Oberon. "Your original
three wishes have been watered until we
find in going over our books for the second
year that they reach the sum total of three
million five hundred and sixty-nine thousand four hundred and thirty-seven, and
that you still have an unexpended balance
on hand of four hundred and ninety-seven
thousand three hundred and seventy-four
wishes. The situation is just this," he con-

tinued. "Our company has been kept so busy honoring your drafts that we are threatened with a general strike. We didn't mind building you a château and furbishing up your old chicken-farm, and setting you up for life, but when you enter into negotiations with old John W. Midas to incorporate yourself into a wish trust we feel that the time has come to call a halt. The fairies are honest, and no obligation of theirs will ever be repudiated, but we think that a man who tries to build up a billion-dollar corporation to deal in wishes on an investment of one poached egg is just a leetle unreasonable. Even Rockernegie had a trifle more than a paper of tacks when he founded the iron trust."

"By ginger, Oberon," said Wilbraham, "you are right! I *have* rather put it on to you people and I'm sorry. I wouldn't embarrass you good fairies for anything in the world."

"Good!" cried Oberon, overjoyed. "I

66

thought you would feel that way. Just
think for one moment what it would mean
for us if the Great Wish Syndicate were
started as a going concern, with a board of
directors made up of men like John W.
Midas, Rockernegie, and old Bondifeller
running things. Why, there aren't fairies
enough in the world to keep up with those
men, and the whole business world would
come down with a crash. Their wish would
elect a whole Congress. If they wished the
Senate out of Washington and located on
Wall Street, you'd soon find it so, and, by
thunder, Wilbraham, every four years they'd
wish somebody in the White House with a
great capacity for taking orders and not
enough spine to fill an umbrella cover, and
the public would be powerless."

Wilbraham gazed thoughtfully out of the
window. A dazzling prospect of imperial
proportions loomed up before his vision,
and the temptation was terrible, but in the
end common sense came to the rescue.

67

"It would be a terrible nuisance," he muttered to himself, and then turning to Oberon he asked: "What is your proposition?"

"A compromise," said the fairy. "If you'll give up your right to further wishes on our account we will place you in a position where, for the rest of your natural life, you will always have four dollars more than you need, and in addition to that, as a compliment to Mrs. Wilbraham, she can have everything she wants."

"Ha!" said Wilbraham, dubiously. "I —I don't think I'd like that exactly. She might want something I didn't want her to have."

"Very well, then," said the fairy, with a broad smile. "We'll make you the flat proposition—you give us a quit-claim deed to all your future right, title, and interest in our wishes, and we will guarantee that as long as you live you will, upon every occasion, find in your pocket five dollars more than you need."

"Make it seven and I'll go you!" cried Wilbraham, really enthusiastic over the suggestion.

"Sure!" returned Oberon with a deep sigh of relief.

"Well, dearest," said Wilbraham that night as he sat down at his onyx dinner-table, "I've gone out of the wish business."

His wife's eyes lit up with a glow of happiness.

"You have?" she cried, delightedly.

"Yes," said Wilbraham; and then he told her of Oberon's call, and the new arrangement, and was rejoiced beyond measure to receive her approval of it.

"I am so glad, Richard," she murmured, with a sigh of content. "I have been kept so busy for two years trying to think of new things to wish for that I have had no time to enjoy all the beautiful things we have."

"And it isn't bad to have seven dollars more than you need whenever you need it, is it, dearest?"

"Bad, Richard?" she returned. "Bad? I should say not, my beloved. To have seven dollars more than you need at all times is, to my mind, the height of an ideal prosperity. I need five thousand dollars at this very minute to pay my milliner's bill."

"And here it is," said her husband, taking five crisp one-thousand-dollar bills from his vest pocket and handing them to her. "And here are seven brand-new ones besides. The fairies are true to their bargain."

And they lived affluently forever afterward, although Midas and his confrères did sue Wilbraham for a hundred million dollars for breach of contract, securing judgment for twenty-nine million dollars, the which Wilbraham paid before leaving the court-room, departing therefrom with a

WILBRAHAM PAID BEFORE LEAVING THE COURT-ROOM

balance of one five and two one dollar bills to the good.

And that is why, my dear children, when you see the Wilbraham motor chugging along the highway, if you look closely you will see painted on the door of the car a simple crest, a poached egg *dormant* upon a piece of toast *couchant*, and underneath it, in golden letters on a scroll, the family motto, *Hic semper septimus.*

III

PUSS, THE PROMOTER

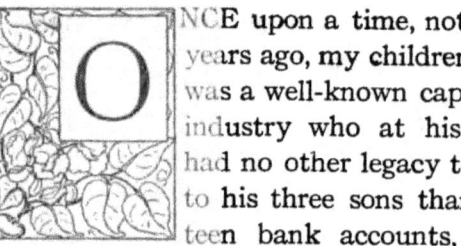NCE upon a time, not many years ago, my children, there was a well-known captain of industry who at his death had no other legacy to leave to his three sons than fourteen bank accounts, all of them overdrawn, a couple of automobiles without any tires on their wheels, and an Angora cat which had taken several prizes at the annual cat show in New York, and upon more than one occasion had had its picture printed in the society columns of the Sunday newspapers.

The eldest son took over the bank accounts, and by the negotiation of several large checks among his friends, each one dated several months ahead, had managed to escape to Venezuela with a comfortable fortune, where, after several revolutions, he found himself in the President's cabinet as Secretary of the Treasury. He further enriched himself in this office by the private sale of national bonds to innocent investors, prior to his departure for Algiers, and became, before his death, a leading spirit in that interesting colony, and an influential member of the Missionary Society of East Africa.

The second son took the automobiles, and with a pot of paint and eight old life-preservers, relics of the palmy days when his father was a famous yachtsman, so furbished them up that he was able to sell them f. o. b. to a couple of farmers in central Connecticut for five thousand dollars, which he invested in Steel Common when it was sulking along between 10 and 12 on a margin of five per cent., and, selling out at 84⅞, he was soon able to retire to the serene joys and quiet pleasures of the Great White Way, along whose verdured slopes he pranked and played until paresis called him at the ripe age of twenty-seven years. But to the youngest son, poor Jack Dinwiddie, by the terms of his father's will, fell only the residue of the estate after the two brothers had had their shares; in other words, the Angora cat!

It was, indeed, a melancholy situation, for poor Jack, like a great many other sons of men of presumably large wealth, had studied only political economy at college, and of the domestic variety knew nothing. He was an honorary member of the Consumers' League, but of the methods of the Producers' Union he knew little, and here at the age of twenty-two he found himself fatherless, penniless, and without any visible means of support in the line of earning capacity.

PUSS, THE PROMOTER

"Well, Puss," he said, gloomily, as he gazed at his Angora cat, who was sitting on top of a pile of unpaid bills in Jack's bachelor apartment, washing his face with his right paw, "it looks to me as if we were up against it. The governor has gone to his last account, my allowance has ceased, and you are the only clear and unencumbered asset in my possession, barring this last cigarette and two matches loaned to me by a kind gentleman upon the street to whom I applied recently for a light."

He paused and lit the cigarette, while Puss, unmindful of the pathos of the situation, continued his prinking, giving especial attention to his whiskers, brushing them upward from his lips until he bore a not very remote resemblance to the Kaiser himself.

"I suppose I could sell you, Bill," the young man went on. "Angora cats, with a pedigree dating back to Dick Whittington's time and a bunch of blue ribbons big enough to supply every prohibitionist in the Union with a bowknot for the lapel of his coat, must have some market value, especially in a time like this, when anything resembling beef is worth its weight in radium; but I won't do it, old man. You've been a mighty good cat to me, and as long as there is a drop of chalk and water left in this world you shall have your morning dish of milk."

It was then that a very singular thing happened.

"That's all I wanted to know, Jack," purred the cat, jumping to the floor and rubbing his sleek sides up against his master's leg affectionately. "If we are not to be separated, it is up to me to show myself the worthy descendant of a noble and resourceful ancestry. There is a tradition in our family that no backyard fence has ever been so hard to climb that we couldn't get over it. Do you know who I am?"

"Why, yes," said Jack, rubbing his eyes in astonishment, for he had never heard the cat speak before. "You are Angora Bill,

78

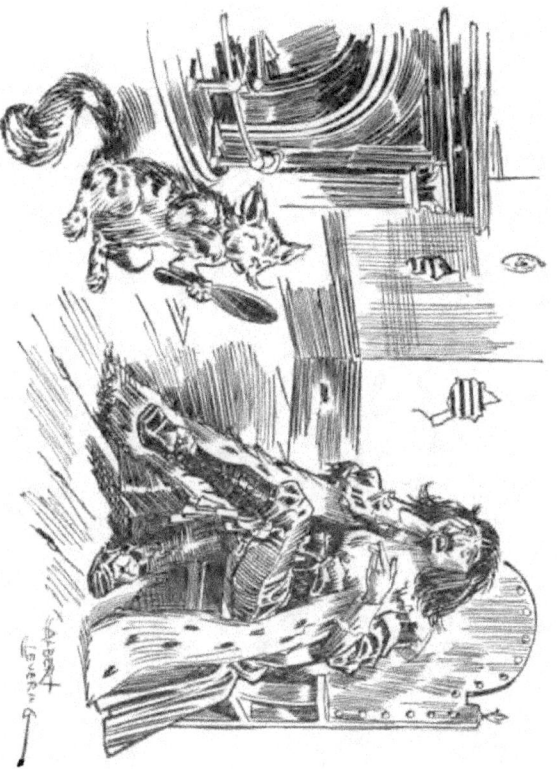

" I SUPPOSE I COULD SELL YOU, BILL "

the Champion Chinchilla of fourteen con-
secutive annual shows, and the neatest little
ratter that ever lived."

"I am more than that," replied the cat,
proudly. "I am the direct lineal descendant
of the original Puss in Boots, and one of the
advance agents of prosperity."

Jacked laughed even in his misery.

"Those days have gone, Puss," he said,
wearily. "There are no longer any fairies
to help poor beggars like me out of a hole,
Bill—"

"That's what you think," smiled puss,
scratching his left ear with his right hind-
paw; "but, my dear boy, my great-great-
great-great-grandfather was a back-fence
piker alongside of myself, who, all unknown
to you, am one of the board of directors of
the United States Fairy Company, of 3007
Wall Street, New York. If you will do just
what I tell you, my boy, we shall emerge
from this little embarrassment of ours with
flying colors, and spend our declining years

6   81

in a little onyx bungalow on the corner of
Bond Avenue and Easy Street that will
make the Vandergilt palace up on the Plaza
look like a particularly cheap and self-
effacing owl-wagon."

Jack gazed mournfully at his companion.
Surely, he thought, our misfortunes have
driven him crazy. Nevertheless he decided
to humor the creature.

"What would you have me do, Puss?" he
asked.

"Nothing much," replied the cat. "Just
pack your suit-case with your few remaining
collars and other garments, fill your five
trunks with Sunday newspapers and unpaid
bills, and move at once into the Waldorf-
Astoria, taking a suite of five rooms and a
bath."

"On nothing?" demanded the astonished
youth.

"You lose less on nothing than you would
if you had something to lose," retorted puss,
with a wise air. "Do as I say. Lend me

a pair of your boots, a derby hat, and your
fur-lined ulster, and wait for me in your
apartment. Go at once to the hotel, register, and ask if there are any letters or messages for you, and all will be well. You
might register as Horace Vanderpoel, of
Cincinnati, or St. Louis, or any other old
place at a comfortable distance from New
York. Let your luggage precede you."

The cat spoke in a masterful tone that inspired confidence. As he delivered his instructions he donned his master's boots and
fur-lined overcoat, and then putting the
derby hat jauntily upon his head he saun-
tered forth.

"Good-bye, Jack," he said, as he reached
the door. "Follow my instructions to the
very last detail, and before long you'll be
wearing diamonds that will make the average incandescent electric light look like an
eclipse."

Now Jack was a venturesome youth and
ready at all times for any kind of an

unusual experience; so, deeply impressed by the mere fact of the cat's having spoken at all, he decided to follow out his instructions to the letter. His five trunks, filled to the brim with papers and bills and any other objects of *virtu* that came handy, were dispatched at once to the Waldorf, and in about three hours he himself followed them, registering in a large, bold hand as Horace Vanderpoel, of Kansas City, in the hotel book.

"I want a suite of five rooms and a bath," said Jack.

"Certainly, Mr. Vanderpoel," said the room-clerk, courteously. "We had already made a reservation for you, sir. We will give you suite number forty-two on the first floor."

"Good!" said Jack. "I wasn't aware that my coming had been heralded—in fact, I have been wanting to have it kept as quiet as possible. Important negotiations, you know."

"We quite understand, Mr. Vanderpoel," said the clerk.

"Have any letters or telephone messages been received for me?" Jack demanded.

"No letters, sir," replied the clerk, "but—er—Mr. Rockernegie's secretary 'phoned us about an hour ago requesting us to ask you to let him know the minute you arrived—fact is, sir, that is how we came to be on the lookout for you."

"Rockernegie, eh?" said Jack, scratching his head with a puzzled air. "Well," he added with a laugh, "I guess he can wait a bit. Have J. W. Midas & Co. rung me up yet?"

"Not yet, sir," said the clerk.

"Well, I'm going down-stairs to be shaved," said Jack. "If Midas does ring me up let me know."

He chuckled as he went down to the barber-shop.

"Bill is a great cat," he muttered to himself. "Rockernegie! Gee! Here's hoping he won't forget Midas and Bondifeller."

He sat down in the barber's chair and was soon richly lathered. The barber was about to apply the razor, when a small boy clad in a perfect rash of buttons entered the shop.

"NUMBER FORTY-TWO, please!" he cried. "Gentleman number FORTY-TWO!"

"Wait a minute, Barber," said Jack. "That's my number. Here, boy, what is it?"

"Wanted on the telephone, sir," said the boy.

"Find out who it is," said Jack, impatiently.

"Yes, sir," said the boy. "I have, sir. They told me to tell you, sir, that Mr. Bondifeller was on the 'phone, sir."

"Oh, is that all?" grinned Jack. "Well, you tell 'em to tell Mr. Bondifeller that I am too busy just at present to see him. You might tell him, too, that I haven't any-

"TELL 'EM TO TELL MR. BONDIFELLER THAT I AM
TOO BUSY TO SEE HIM"

thing to add to what I said in my last letter. If he doesn't like that, the deal is off."

There was a considerable craning of necks in the neighboring chairs, for Jack had not thought to address his remarks to the lad in tones suggestive of a confidential communication. The boy staggered slightly on his feet, but managed to get away without dropping under the weight of such a message, and Jack, lying back in his chair, requested the barber to proceed.

"Bill is a great cat!" he chuckled.

"Beg pardon?" queried the barber.

"I say don't shave me too close," said Jack.

The shave over, Jack retired to his apartment and found in suite number forty-two everything that the heart of man could desire, and throughout the great caravansary the name of Horace Vanderpoel was held in high honor. To be sure they had never heard of him before, but the associate of these brilliant dignitaries of the financial world must indeed be somebody, even in New York! Here he sat, awaiting developments, his amusement as well as his interest in the adventure increasing momentarily. An hour passed and then a card was brought to his door bearing the mystic words:

COLONEL A. N. GORA

The Catskill Club

"Ask Colonel Gora to come right up, said Jack, with difficulty repressing the guffaw that struggled within him for expression, recognizing the name at once. Five minutes later puss walked in, the perfect picture of a military dandy, largely due no doubt to the cut of his whiskers.

"Well," he said, removing his gloves, and out of sheer force of habit proceeding to wash his face with his right paw, "you seem to be pretty comfortably located."

"In the lap of luxury," grinned Jack.

Puss's face grew solemn.

"For a cat, my dear Jack, or, rather, Horace," he said, "the lap of luxury would be a saucer of milk."

"You shall have a pitcherful, Bill," cried Jack, rushing to the 'phone.

"Not on your life, my dear boy!" meowed puss, excitedly stopping him. "Never! The occupant of an apartment like this ordering a pitcher of milk! Why, my dear fellow, that would queer our game at the very start. Order some tea and I'll drink the cream."

After regaling himself on the refreshment provided by the confiding management, puss, with a graceful readjustment of his whiskers, turned with a smile to the wondering and admiring beneficiary of his resourceful mind.

"Well, what do you think of it, Jack?" he asked.

"It is very nice indeed, Puss," Jack answered, "but—er—I can't help thinking of the possibilities of the day of reckoning. Who's going to pay for all this when the bill comes in?"

"Don't worry," said puss; "I'll attend to all that. This afternoon I want you to climb aboard the sight-seeing coach that leaves Madison Square at three o'clock. Sit next to the young lady with blue eyes and a Persian lamb ulster, whom you will find occupying the front seat with her father, a large, stout gentleman with a kohinoor sparkling like an electric light in his shirt-front and three more on his little finger. If you happen to see me on the same coach, don't let on that you know me, and, above all, don't deny anything you may hear anybody saying about you. Where did you register from?"

"Kansas City," replied Jack.

"All right," said puss. "Keep a stiff upper lip, my boy, and all will be well. Good-bye. Like most cats, I have a few

"GOOD-BYE, JACK"

fences to take care of this afternoon and I
must be off. I've found a nice little
kitten up the street who is going to mani-
cure my nails."

With these words the amazing creature
donned his hat and coat and, resuming his
boots, strode out with a magnificent swagger.

At three o'clock in the afternoon Jack, in
accordance with his instructions, boarded
the sight-seeing coach at Madison Square,
and, recognizing the young woman referred
to by puss sitting on the front seat of the
car, seated himself beside her.

"When do we start, Popper?" asked the
girl, with a demure glance at Jack.

"Putty soon, I guess," said the old gentleman, who sat on her other side. "But there
ain't never any tellin'. These New York
guys does things putty much as they please."

"Humph!" muttered Jack under his
breath. "He sounds like real money from
Goldfields."

In a few moments the car started, and as

they passed around the Flatiron Building Jack was still further amazed to recognize in the voice of the lecturer none other than that of the faithful puss.

"This building," Jack heard him saying boldly, "is the famous Flatiron Building, erected at great expense by the Fuller Company and lately purchased for five million dollars by the famous Missouri financier and capitalist, Mr. Horace Vanderpoel."

"*Gee-rusalem!*" ejaculated Jack.

"To the right is the wonderful tower of the Metropolitan Life Insurance Building— the handsomest tower in the world," continued puss, bellowing his words into Jack's ears playfully through his megaphone; "while off across the square to the north the structure in yellow brick is the famous Madison Square Garden, soon to be torn down to make room for the new Vanderpoel office building, sixty-four stories high, containing theatres, assembly halls, churches, convention halls, restaurants, apartments, and so on, besides offices, costing between ten and twenty millions of dollars."

"Vanderpoel Building, eh?" said the old gentleman. "Any relation to the feller that's bought the Flatiron?"

"Same man, sir. He's the only Vanderpoel," replied puss.

"Must have seven or eight dollars to spare," said the sight-seer.

"Ten or twelve, sir," laughed puss. "It is said that he is trying to buy a controlling interest in the whole city. Negotiating for the Astor estate, they say."

"Great Scott!" gasped the sight-seer. "What's he going to do with it when he gets it?"

"Don't know, sir," replied puss, gayly. "Kind of suspect he's thinking of annexing it to Kansas City, sir."

The car proceeded until the party reached the Plaza.

"On the left is the Plaza Hotel, another property of the Vanderpoel syndicate," said

7 97

puss; "said to have cost the Kansas City millionaire ten millions, and paid for in cash."

"*Gee!*" gasped the young woman's father, and Jack indorsed the observation unreservedly.

"That's a pretty house, Popper," said the young woman as the car reached the Ninety-sixth Street entrance to the Park, pointing toward Mr. Rockernegie's residence.

"Formerly the residence of Andrew Rockernegie," said puss, "but recently sold to Mr. Vanderpoel for three million dollars."

"It's mighty funny I never heard of this Vanderpoel feller before," said the old man.

"Just come into his fortune, sir," vouchsafed puss. "Very young man just come of age, sir."

The old man leaned forward and, addressing Jack, inquired:

"Did you ever hear of this man Vanderpoel, young man?"

"Well, yes," said Jack, with a modest

"THE HANDSOMEST TOWER IN THE WORLD"

laugh. "Fact is, *I myself am Horace Van-derpoel*."

The stranger gazed at him in amazement.

"Well, by ginger!" he said. "I—I—I'm dee-lighted to meet you, sir. This is my daughter Amanda, sir. I—I—I'm proud to make your acquaintance."

"It is a pleasure to meet you, sir," said Jack, pleasantly, removing his hat and bowing to the young woman. "You are Mr.—"

"Dobbins, sir," returned the old man, effusively. "Joshua Dobbins. I thought I was going some on the money question, with seven gold mines in Nevada, but I must take off my hat to you, sir. Any man who has the nerve to buy New York— heavens!"

The old fellow took off his hat and mopped his brow, which had begun to perspire freely.

"Oh, I don't take any credit to myself for that," said Jack, modestly. "When a boy has a great-grandfather who dies and leaves forty million dollars to him in trust for fifty years before he was born, and that money accumulates until the unborn beneficiary is twenty-one years old, it means a rather tidy stockingful, I admit, but it isn't as if I'd made the money myself."

" Fuf-forty million accumulating interest for seventy-one years!" gasped Dobbins.

"Compound," said Jack, smiling sweetly at the girl at his side. "That's the deuce of it. I—I've got to do something to keep the income invested, and New York real estate, being the most expensive thing in sight, I've gone in for that as being the easiest way out."

"I—I suppose you are living here now?" asked Mr. Dobbins.

"No," said Jack. "Personally I don't care particularly for New York. I am just in town for a few days, stopping at the Waldorf."

"Why, so are we," interrupted the girl.

"Then," said Jack, gallantly, "the Wal-dorf possesses even greater attractions than I had supposed."

The girl blushed a rosy red, and the old gentleman fairly beamed.

"Glad to have you take dinner with us, Mr. Vanderpoel," he said.

"Thank you," said Jack. "I shall be charmed to do so if I can. I sort of half promised Mr. Bondifeller to take a snack with him this evening, but"—this with a killing glance at the blushing Miss Dobbins —"but I guess he can wait. To tell you the truth, Mr. Dobbins, these New York mil-lionaires bore me to death. At what time shall we foregather?"

"Suppose we say seven?" said the old gentleman.

"My lucky number," said Jack, with a gracious smile, which set the heart of Miss Dobbins all of a-flutter.

So passed the hours away. Jack found himself growing momentarily more deeply impressed with the beauty of the maiden at his side, and by the time the young people had reached the hotel it had become a pronounced case of pure and ardent love. As they entered the Waldorf one of the employees of the hotel rushed excitedly up to the young billionaire, breathless with the importance of a communication intrusted to him.

"Mr. Rockernegie is on the wire—wants to speak to you immediately, sir," he panted.

"Tell him I'm busy," said Jack, entering the tea-room and ordering a slight repast for Miss Dobbins and her father. A moment later the messenger returned, more breathless than before.

"Sorry, sir," said the boy, "but Mr. Rockernegie says he must see you right away, sir."

Jack frowned as though deeply annoyed, and his answer came with an incisive coldness that froze Mr. Dobbins almost to the marrow.

"Go back to that 'phone and tell the gentleman that it will take the biggest search-light in the amalgamated navies of the world to enable him to get even a bird's-eye view of me until I get good and ready," he said. "Er—tell him he can come to my office at ten-thirty to-morrow morning if he wants to, only he mustn't be late. Just impress that on his mind."

Mr. Dobbins choked and coughed apoplectically.

"Don't let us interfere with any of your engagements, Mr. Vanderpoel," he sputtered.

"That's all right, Mr. Dobbins," said Jack.

"I wish you'd invest seven or eight million for me," said Dobbins, with a sheepish glance at Jack. "I know it isn't much, but—"

"Risky business, speculating, Mr. Dobbins," said Jack, bravely, although the suggestion had nearly knocked him off his chair. "Better hang on to your pennies, now that you've got 'em."

"Oh, I've got eight or ten more where they came from," chuckled the old man.

"Then, sir," said Jack, as calmly as he knew how, "the best investment for you is in Miss Amanda Dobbins Preferred, a stock of priceless value."

"I don't think I quite understand," said the old man, scratching his head in perplexity.

"Settle five million on your daughter," explained Jack. "When you've got her fixed comfortably in life, go in and do as you please with the rest of your fortune. Play the game as hard as you like, and, win or lose, no harm can come to her—and *if* you lose, why, she'll be able to take care of you."

"I've already given her four million, haven't I, Amandy?" said the old gentleman, proudly.

"Yes, Popper," said the girl, and Jack's

"COULDN'T MAKE IT THREE MILLION, COULD YOU?" SUGGESTED MR. DOBBINS

heart began to play the anvil chorus on the xylophone of his ribs.   What a chance!

"How about it, Mr. Vanderpoel," persisted the old man; "can you put me wise?"

"Oh, well," said Jack, "if you really insist I'll let you into a little blind pool I'm in, but not for very much—say a couple of millions.   Only I won't take a penny of your money if you are like all the rest of these people here who want to be shown how things are every five minutes of the day. I'll take your two million and you can call it a loan, if you want to.   Your receipt will be my demand note for the full amount.   You see I know what I'm about, and I'm careful."

"Couldn't make it three million, could you?" suggested Mr. Dobbins, with a pleading note in his voice which Jack found difficult to resist.   "I happen to have that amount idle—"

"Well, I'll tell you what I'll do," said Jack, patronizingly.   "I was going to pull this thing off myself because it is one of the few dead-sure things left in this world, but first the Midas people butted in, then Bondifeller wanted a slice, and Rockernegie wore out his library carpet running to the 'phone to ring me up about it, until I told Central I'd have the company indicted as a nuisance if they let the old man have my number again. None the less, for merely diplomatic reasons, I'm going to let 'em all in for a small share. Just enough to keep them satisfied with themselves. Exactly what the basis will be I haven't yet decided, but if you are willing to take your chances with them—well, you may hand me six certified checks for five hundred thousand dollars apiece, so that I can spread the whole amount around in my various bank and trust company accounts."

"Now what, Puss?" asked Jack the next afternoon, as he and his feline friend held a consultation in the apartment. "I've got three million to my credit in six banks. What's the next step — Algiers or Venezuela?"

"Why," said puss, "it seems to me that a man with three million in hand can afford to stay in New York over Christmas, anyhow."

"Yes, I know," said Jack. "But the old man—he's got to have some profit some time or other, hasn't he?"

Puss sighed deeply. "It is very evident, my dear Jack," said he, "that you are no financier. Settle a million on yourself and use the remainder to pay dividends to Mr. Dobbins. He'd probably think twenty-five per cent. on his investment was a pretty fair return, and if at the end of the first year you give him back seven hundred and fifty thousand dollars he'll be satisfied. Then if you hand him over a full million the second year—well—"

"Well what?" gasped Jack.

"He'll put five million more into the pool

on your mere intimation that you are willing to help him out to that extent," said puss, "which will keep you going several years longer."

Jack breathed heavily at the prospect of such affluence, but he could not escape the uncomfortable feeling that there would be an inevitable day of reckoning ahead of him.

"And when that is gone?" he asked.

Puss gazed at him scornfully this time.

"My, but you are stupid!" he ejaculated. "I really want to help you, Jack, but I can't do everything, you know. You've got to handle some of this business yourself. But let me ask you one question: Did you ever hear of a millionaire putting the father of his grandchildren in jail because he had lost money in a blind speculation?"

"No, I never did," said Jack; "but you see, Puss, I am not the father of Dobbins' grandchildren."

"No," said puss, "but why in thunder should you not be?"

"By Jove!" cried Jack, joyously. "Do you think she'll have me?"

"Will a duck quack?" asked the cat.

(Extract from the last will and testament of Joshua Dobbins):

". . . and I do hereby appoint my said son-in-law, Horace Vanderpoel, husband of my beloved daughter Amanda, sole trustee of my estate, without bond, said estate to be administered by him for the benefit of my said daughter Amanda and her children, according to his own discretion; for which service, in lieu of executor's or trust fees, I do hereby give, bequeath, and devise to his use forever the sum of five million dollars, together with such additional sums as I have from time to time during the past four years invested under his advice and direction in the several properties in his control, both principal and interest accrued up to the date of my decease."

"Dear old dad!" said Jack, when the will had been read. "Your father was a fine man, Amanda dear, and a very successful man as well."

"Yes, Horace," said his weeping wife,

"but he always insisted that he owed much to your splendid business management; so, after all, you have only come into your own, dear."

"Ah, well," said Jack, as he opened a fresh bottle of cream and placed it before his pet Angora, "money isn't everything, sweetheart, and I should have been satisfied if he had left me nothing but you."

And the Angora cat wiped off the back of his ear with his left paw and twirled his mustachios upward with a wave of his right, as he purred amiably over the cream.

IV

THE GOLDEN FLEECE

T HERE was once a miller who was very poor, but he had a beautiful daughter. There were a great many people who said that if he had not had so beautiful a daughter he would not have been so poor, and it may be that these were right, for beautiful daughters are not infrequently a source of considerable expense to their parents, and I fear me that Gasmerilda was no exception to this rule.

She had a great passion for rare furs and for opera and lingerie cloaks, and the thousand and one other dainty things that appeal to the heart of beautiful young maiden-hood, and it seemed to make no difference how many millions of bushels of corn passed through her father's mill day after day, the returns from the grinding wheels were always thirty or forty dollars a month lower than the total aggregate of Gasmerilda's bills from milliners, furriers, jewelers, and others too numerous to mention.

Of course, this thing could not go on indefinitely. There comes a time when even the blindest of creditors will insist upon the liquidation of a miller's account, and the poor man found himself getting deeper and deeper into debt as the months passed along, and was now at last at his wits' ends to devise new excuses for the non-payment of Gasmerilda's indebtedness. Indeed, he had now come to a point where there was but one refuge from the ultimate of financial disaster that should force him into a public declaration of his bankruptcy, and that was to be seen associating in public places with well - known malefactors of great wealth.

What awful agony of mind this cost him —for he was an honest miller, as had always been evidenced by his willingness to promise to pay his debts even when he knew he could not—the world will never know, but he swallowed his pride, and for a time gained immunity from the pressure of his creditors with their threatened judgments by being seen walking down Fifth Avenue in the morning alongside of Colonel John W. Midas, the president of the Pactolean Trust Company, a savings institution formed . primarily for the purpose of lending its depositors' money to members of its own board of directors, taking their checks dated two months ahead and indorsed by their office-boys and stenographers for security.

It is true that anybody who was ever seen speaking to Colonel Midas in public was, by orders of the district attorney, immediately snap-shotted by the Secret Ser-

vice Camera Squad attached to that gentleman's office, and the resulting negatives
filed away for future reference in case Justice should ever, by some odd chance, peep
over the top of her bandage for a moment
and fix her eagle eye upon the Colonel's
doings; but, on the other hand, there were
countless thousands of worthy people, and
among them were the miller's creditors,
who believed that association with such a
person as Colonel Midas was pretty good
evidence either of a man's solvency or of
his immunity to the lash of the law. Con-
sequently, when for five successive morn-
ings the furriers, the jewelers, the milliners,
and others, to whom the unfortunate miller
owed vast unpayable sums of money for
sundries purchased from time to time by
the beautiful Gasmerilda, saw their debtor
walking down-town alongside of the great
Pactolean magnate, they called off their
collectors and attorneys, and sent the beautiful girl extra notifications through the

mails of their new fall and winter importa-
tions; to which, in due course of time, the
lovely maid responded, to the consequent
swelling of the already over-large accounts
due.   If these persons had only known that
these walks upon the avenue were silent
walks, and that from the Plaza down to
Madison Square Colonel Midas, though ac-
companied by the miller, was utterly un-
aware of the latter's presence, being too
deeply absorbed in certain operations of
great magnitude upon the Street to notice
anything that was going on around him,
they would doubtless have acted differently;
but they did not know this, and it soon
passed about among the tradesmen that the
miller was the friend of Midas, and thereby
was his credit greatly expanded.

On the morning of the sixth day's prom-
enade, however, Colonel Midas, having solved
the particular problem upon which his mind
had been set for the past week or ten days,
became more observant, and, after the mil-

ler had walked at his side for several blocks, he remarked the fact, and with emotions that were not altogether pleasant. Wherefore, he quickened his footsteps in order that he might leave the intruder behind, but the miller quickened his also and remained alongside. Colonel Midas stopped short in his walk before an art-shop window, and gazed in at the paintings therein displayed.

The miller likewise, his head cocked knowingly to one side like that of a connoisseur, paused and gazed in at the marvels of the brush. The Colonel, with a sudden jerky turn, leaped from the window to the gutter-curb and boarded a moving omnibus with surprising agility for a man of his years. But he was not too quick for his pursuer, for the miller, though scarcely able to afford the expense, immediately sprang aboard the same vehicle and took the seat beside him. Then for the first time the Colonel addressed him, and, there being no ladies upon the

"WHAT DO YOU THINK YOU ARE DOING?"

omnibus at that early hour, in terms rather more forcible than polite.

"What do you think you are doing?" he demanded, frowning upon his pursuer.

"Riding in a 'bus," replied the miller, with a pleasant smile.

"Are you trying to shadow me?" roared the Colonel.

"I'd make a mighty poor eclipse for you, Colonel Midas," said the miller, suavely, "but to tell you the truth," he added, a sudden idea having flashed across his mind, which in the absence of anything else to say in explanation of his conduct seemed as good as any other excuse he could invent, "there *is* a little matter I'd like to bring to your attention."

"Bombs?" asked the Colonel, moving away apprehensively, noticing that the miller had put his hand into his pocket, and fearing that he had, perhaps, encountered a crank who designed to do him harm.

"No, indeed," laughed the miller. "Not

in such close quarters as this. When I throw a bomb at anybody I shall take care to provide a safety net for myself."

"Ha!" ejaculated the Colonel, with a deep sigh of relief. "Book-agent?"

"Nothing in it," said the miller. "Work too heavy for the profits. No, sir, I am neither a book-agent nor an anarchist. I am nothing but a poor miller with an in-growing income, but I have a beautiful daughter who—"

"Oh yes," interrupted Midas, with a nod. "I remember now. I've heard of you. You preferred to remain independent instead of selling out to the Trust. You tried to discount some of your notes at the Pactolean Trust Company, of which I am president, the other day."

"Yes," said the miller, "and you refused them."

"Naturally," laughed Midas. "A beautiful daughter, Mr. Miller, is a lovely possession, but she's mighty poor security for a loan. About the worst in the market. Especially yours. I've seen Miss Miller at the opera several times and have wondered how you managed it. It would cost more than the face value of your notes to support the security for one week in the style to which she is accustomed."

"That's true enough," said the miller, "and nobody knows it better than I do. Nevertheless, you made a mistake. You have possibly never heard of her wonderful gift."

"No," said the magnate. "I was not aware that the young lady had any other gifts than beauty and a father with a little credit left."

"Well, be that as it may," retorted the miller, "she has one great gift. She can spin straw into gold."

"What?" cried Midas, becoming interested at once.

"Yes, sir," the miller went on. "She has marvellous powers in that direction. If she hadn't I'd have been up a tree long ago."

"I had heard of her father's ability to turn hot air into Russian sables and diamond necklaces, but this straw business is something new," said Midas.

"I thought you would so regard it," said the miller, confidently, "and that is why I have been trying to get a word with you for the past week. You are the only man I know in the financial world who is known to have the enterprise and the courage to go into a little gamble that other people would laugh at. You have that prime quality of success, Colonel Midas, that is known to mankind as nerve. You are always willing to sit in any kind of a game that shows a glimmer of profit in the perspective, and that is why I bring this matter to you instead of to my friend Rockernegie, a man utterly without imagination and blind to many a sure thing because he can't understand it."

The Colonel, who was not unsusceptible

to flattery, was visibly impressed by this
tribute. He scratched his head thoughtfully for a moment.

"See here, Mr. Miller," he said, after a
brief communion with himself, "if this story
is true, why are you trying to discount your
notes at the Pactolean Trust Company?
Why don't you get a bale of straw and have
your daughter turn it over a few times?"

"I will be perfectly frank with you,
Colonel," said the miller. "It is a humiliat-
ing confession to make, sir, but I'm ever-
lastingly busted. Just plain down and out
and I couldn't buy a lemonade straw if they
were going at a cent a ton, much less a bale."

The Colonel looked at him sympathetically, and then, giving his knee a resounding
whack, he cried: "By Jove, Miller, I'll back
you! I rather like your nerve, and, as you
have so charmingly put it, I *am* the sort of
man to take a long shot. Yes, sir, and I
wouldn't have had seven cents to my name
to-day if I hadn't been. Come with me to

the Pactolean Trust Company and we'll discount your demand note, suitably indorsed, right off, with the understanding, however, that your daughter gives us an immediate demonstration of her powers. We'll furnish the straw."

The miller's heart leaped with joy, but he deemed it well not to show himself overanxious lest he lose the whole advantage.

"It is very good of you, Colonel," he observed quietly, "but I don't know a soul in this bright, beautiful world who would indorse my note for any sum, large or small."

"Oh, that will be all right," laughed the Colonel. "We've got a rubber stamp in the office for just such emergencies."

So the miller and his new-found friend went to the offices of the Pactolean Trust Company, where, in a short while, he found relief from his pressing woes by the exchange of his demand note for five thousand dollars, indorsed most appropriately by a man of straw, for four crisp one-thousand-dollar treasury notes and the balance, less six months' interest, in yellow-backs of a denomination of fifty dollars each.

"Tell your daughter to come down here to-morrow morning," said the Colonel, as the miller pocketed the money. "I'll summon the board of directors and she can give us a demonstration of her gift in the private office. We'll have a couple of bales of straw all ready for her."

"You will have to excuse me, Colonel," said the miller, with that calmness which a man is likely to show when he has five thousand dollars in good money in his purse, "but that will be impossible. Gasmerilda has always refused to exercise her gift in the presence of anybody else, and I am quite sure she will make no exception in this case. Even as a child she would not let either her mother or myself see how she did it."

"But she must," said the Colonel, firmly, "or I shall be under the painful necessity of calling that note at once."

"But she can't," returned the miller. "You see, sir, it is one of the peculiarities of the gift that she must be alone while at work. It requires such intense concentration of effort. If you insist upon her presence here, why—well, as you intimate, the deal is off between us and I shall have to take it to Rockernegie. There's the money, sir."

With a supreme effort of will the miller tossed the roll of bills back upon the table. It was, of course, an act of sheer bravado, but he carried it off so well that it worked.

"Oh, very well," said the Colonel, gruffly, a shade of disappointment crossing his face. "If she can't, she can't, I suppose. It's worth a try, anyhow. We'll send a bale of straw up to your residence this afternoon, and if by to-morrow morning she has managed to turn it into gold, all well and good. If not—well, we call the note, that's all."

"Can't you make it a week?" pleaded the miller. "She may have some other engage-

"THERE'S THE MONEY, SIR"

ment on for to-night, and—er—well, a week will give her time to turn around."

"Make it five days," said the Colonel. "To-day is Wednesday. Let her make the delivery on Monday morning."

"Done!" said the miller, overjoyed, and he went out.

He had not the slightest notion in the world how his beautiful daughter would be able to fulfil the agreement—indeed, he was fairly certain in his mind that she would be able to do nothing of the sort, but he had the use of five thousand dollars at a critical moment in his career and he knew that if worst came to worst he could shave off his mustache, and, thus disguised, take passage for Europe in the steerage of some one of the many Saturday steamers.

Now, on his return home that evening, the miller was very much embarrassed by a searching inquiry from his beautiful daughter. It seems that when she had tried to telephone to one of her friends that afternoon she had been informed by Central that the service had been discontinued for non-payment of the bill for December, 1906.

"Have we come to such a pass as that, father?" she demanded, her lovely voice quivering with emotion.

"It looks like it," said the miller, with an uneasy laugh. "I have been kept so busy paying for your daily supply of fresh sables that I haven't had a moment for the gas bills or for your conversational accounts. With you to look after, my dear, I find that even talk is not cheap."

The beautiful girl wiped the tears from her eyes with her point-lace handkerchief.

"But," she cried, "what are we going to do? I must have eleven hundred and seventy dollars and fifty-five cents to-morrow morning, father, or I shall be ruined."

The miller's heart sank within him and his face grew ashen.

"Eleven hundred and seventy dollars and

fuf-fifty—fuf—five cents?" he stammered.
"In Heaven's name what for, Gasmerilda—
hairpins?"

"No, father," she trembled. "I have is-
sued three or four pounds of deferred bridge
certificates, and they fall due to-morrow.
You certainly do not wish me to lose my
social position—about the only thing I have
left?"

The unhappy man gazed long and anx-
iously at the pale face before him, and then
his heart softened, as it always had done.

"All right, my child," he sighed, as he
tossed the exact amount to her across the
table. Then his face grew stern.

"Gasmerilda," he said, "your extrava-
gance having brought us to this, I may as
well inform you now as at any other time
that it is up to you to get us out of trouble,
and I have to-day been forced to enter into
negotiations with the Pactolean Trust Company by which you are to be capitalized.
Hereafter, my child, you are to become a

dividend - paying investment instead of twin sister to a sinking fund."

"What can you mean, father?" cried the girl, her face blanching with fear.

The miller thereupon recounted to her in full detail the incidents of the morning, and revealed to her astounded mind the preposterous claims he had made on her behalf.

"But father," she protested, "I have no such gift."

"You will excuse me for refusing to discuss the matter further with you, Gasmerilda," he replied, coldly. "If it so happens that you have no such gift you must devise some method of getting it. I have given my word, and as a dutiful daughter you must make good."

Turning to the butler, the miller asked:

"James, has a bale of straw arrived here to-day from Colonel Midas?"

"Yes, sir," said the butler. "It is downstairs in the cellar, sir."

"Good!" said the miller. "You will have

POOR GASMERILDA SAT WHITE-FACED

it carried up to Miss Miller's dressing-room at once."

Rising from the table he kissed his unhappy daughter affectionately, and, bidding her good-night, he went to the club, where he paid his delinquent dues and house charges and set out once more upon a tolerably care-free existence for five days at least.

"A short life and a merry one!" he muttered to himself, as he paid in a hundred dollars for a supply of red and blue chips.

Meanwhile, poor Gasmerilda sat white-faced, and eyes wide with fear and perplexity, staring at that horrible bale of straw that occupied the middle of the floor of her dainty boudoir. She had no more idea of how to spin it into gold than she had of making over her last year's gingham bath-robe into a this year's panne-velvet opera gown. Hourly her distress grew, until finally the floodgates of her tears broke, and she burst into a passionate convulsion of weeping.

But, even as the tears began to flow, there came a faint golden tinkle on the jeweled 'phone that stood on her escritoire. At first she paid no attention to the unexpected tintinnabulation, but the tinkling soon became more pronounced and so persistent that she finally answered it.

"Is that you, Gasmerilda?" came a quaint little voice over the wire.

"Yes," she sobbed. "Who is this?"

"There are tears in your voice, Gasmerilda," came the quaint little voice.

"They are all over the place," wept the unhappy girl.

"And I know why," said the little voice, sympathetically. "I am your fairy godmother, Gasmerilda, and I have not ceased to watch over you. Your father has negotiated a loan on your remarkable gift of spinning straw into gold, has he not?"

"Yes," sobbed Gasmerilda, "and I have no such gift."

"Well, don't worry, my child," said the

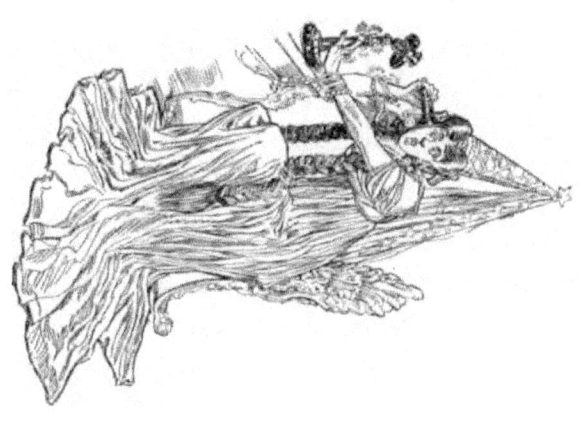

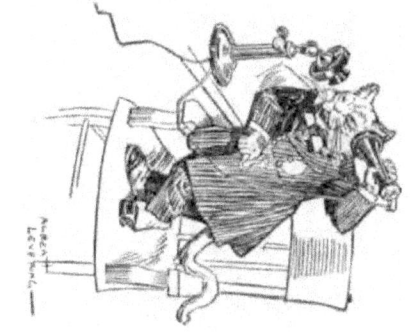

"I AM YOUR FAIRY GODMOTHER, GASMERILDA"

little voice. "When you were a baby you once offered a part of your school orange to a starving kitten, and she has not forgotten it. I was that kitten and I have kept my eye on you ever since, and now I am going to help you out. If you will do exactly what I tell you to do all will be well."

Gasmerilda, with a great sigh of relief, promised to be faithful to her fairy god-mother's instructions.

"Oh, you dear!" she cried, impulsively.

"Go to-morrow, the first thing in the morning," said the fairy godmother, "to the United States Assay Office on Wall Street, taking with you the money your father gave you this evening at dinner, and buy a one-thousand-dollar bar of gold."

"But, Fairy Godmother," Gasmerilda interrupted, "I—I must use that money to pay off my bridge I. O. U.'s to-morrow."

"I have arranged for all that," laughed the fairy godmother. "Those I. O. U.'s will never be presented. Transforming myself into a mouse, I have entered the escritoires of the ladies holding your notes of hand, and have eaten every single one of them.''

Gasmerilda's heart leaped with joy.

"Oh, Fairy Godmother!" she cried. "Can't you get rid of father's note in the same way?"

"No, my dear," sighed the little voice. "That note, unfortunately, is stored away in a steel vault, and my teeth are not strong enough to nibble through that. I have a more business-like method to get you both out of your troubles. After you have purchased the bar of gold, take it home with you and devise some convenient means of getting rid of the straw without anybody seeing you do it. The best way to do this will be to carry an armful of it at a time up on to the roof of your house and let it blow away; and then, when next Monday comes, and your father is required to deliver the first consignment of the precious metal to Colonel Midas, go with him to the Colonel's office,

yourself, taking the gold bar with you, and
see that it is really delivered. Wear your
most bewitching hat, and don't fail to remember what a woman's eyes were given
her for."

"Oh, thank you, thank you, thank you!"
cried Gasmerilda, a great wave of happiness
sweeping over her. "If I could get at you,
dear Fairy Godmother, over the 'phone, I
should hug you to death."

"That is all right, child. My reward will
come later," replied the fairy godmother.
"When your profits begin to come in you
may pay me a commission of ten per cent.
on all you get."

"Gladly. I'll make it fifteen per cent.,"
cried the grateful girl. "But how shall you
be paid?"

"By check, dear, drawn to the order of
The Fairy's Aid Society of America, of which
I am the president," was the answer. "The
address is just Wall Street, New York. And
now, sweet dreams, my beloved ward. The

sun of your troubles has set, and the dawn of prosperity is here."

With a happy smile Gasmerilda wished her kindly friend good-night, and retired to her couch and slept the sleep of a weary child. Bright and early the next morning, with her little gold-chain purse containing the necessary funds dangling from her chatelaine, she appeared at the assay office, and purchased there a shining bar of the lustrous metal, returning to her home in time for luncheon.

"Well, daughter," said the miller, as he met her in the hallway, "how does the good work proceed?"

"Very well, indeed, father," she said, with a cheery smile. "I'm a little out of practise, but I managed to spin about ninety-eight dollars' worth last night before going to bed."

The miller blinked amazedly at his daughter. This answer was indeed the most extraordinary substitute for the floods of tears he had expected to greet his question.

"You—you—you dud—don't—m—m— mean to sus—say—" he stammered.

"Father, dear, did you ever try to cut calves-foot jelly with a steel knife?" she asked.

"Yes, child, yes—but what of that?" he demanded, completely nonplussed.

"Well, dear," she answered, kissing him on the tip end of his nose, "that is hard labor compared to spinning gold out of straw."

She ran from him, laughing merrily as she hurried up the stairs to her room, while he, staggering back against the newel-post of the staircase, leaned on it, breathing heavily.

"If that's the case," he said, as with trembling hands he took a set of false whiskers and a steerage ticket for Naples from his pocket, "I shall not need these."

Nevertheless, prudence bade him wait until he had seen the gold before destroying the paraphernalia of his possible flight, and oh, the joy of that Saturday morning, when Gasmerilda, having, by an almost superhuman effort, having rid herself of the straw as her fairy godmother had bade her to do, led her trembling father into her boudoir and showed him the glittering bar!

"Are you sure it's real?" he quavered.

"I have had it stamped at the assay office, father," she replied. "See!"

And she showed him the stamps of the authorized government test.

"My child!" he cried, dancing about the room in a delirium of joy. "My beloved, my beautiful daughter—was ever miller so blessed as I! Wait!"

Rushing madly to the jeweled 'phone, he rang up Colonel Midas.

"Excuse me for bothering you, Colonel," he said, excitedly, "but this is Miller. I thought you would be interested to know that my daughter has turned the trick a little sooner than I expected. If you want to see the gold to-day instead of waiting until Monday, all you've got to do is to say so."

The wire fairly sizzled with the reply. Of

"THIS IS THE GREATEST CINCH IN THE HISTORY OF FINANCE"

course, Colonel Midas would not wait. In fact, he'd be right up. How much did the miller think the gold would pan out?

"Oh, about a thousand dollars," replied the miller.

"What?" roared Midas. "A thousand dollars' worth of gold from a seven-dollar bub—bale of straw?"

"That's the assay office estimate," said the miller, with a smile. "You can't very well go behind that."

The answer was a long, low whistle, and within twenty minutes the great financier's car came chugging up to the door, and he entered the house, bringing with him a chemist.

"By Jingo! Miller," he cried, after the chemist had applied every known test to the bar and declared it to be, beyond all question, the real stuff, "by Jingo, old man, our fortune is made. This is the greatest cinch in the history of finance."

"Looks that way," said the miller, calmly,

leaning forward and tossing the steerage ticket into the waste-basket.

"We—er—we must keep it in the family, Miller," the Colonel added, slapping the proud father familiarly on the knee—for Gasmerilda had remembered the fairy godmother's injunction as to the use of her eyes.

"I intend to, Colonel," said the miller, dryly. "I'll keep it in *my* family if you don't mind—"

Midas gasped, and then he laughed sheepishly.

"To think that I, a hardened old bachelor, should be a victim to love at first sight!" he said.

"Very funny indeed," laughed the miller.

"What would you say to me as a son-in-law, eh?" Midas went on. "You know I'm a decent chap, old man. No funny business about my private life—it's a good chance to get your daughter settled in life, and—"

"Well, I don't know," said the miller, coolly. "You are generally considered to be a fairly eligible sort of person, Midas, but my daughter can afford to marry for love as long as the straw crop holds good.''

A glitter came into Midas's eye.

"What if I were to corner the market?" he demanded.

"That would be bad for Gasmerilda and me," the miller agreed. "Mind you, I haven't said I disapproved of the match, but let's be perfectly frank with each other. I'm not going to sell my daughter to you or to anybody else, but you know how things run these days. A man's a millionaire to-day and a member of the down-and-out club to-morrow. Now, I don't know the first blessed thing about your prospects. You are rich now, but who knows that before 1915 you won't be in a federal jail somewhere without a nickel?"

"I see your point," said Midas, "and I'll settle five million on her to-morrow."

"Real money?" he demanded.

"Real money," said Midas.

" Done!" ejaculated the miller.

And so the papers settling five million dollars in approved securities upon the miller's daughter were executed, and three months later that invincible old bachelor, John W. Midas, for whom countless widows had set their caps in vain, was led to the altar by the blushing and happy Gasmerilda. The groom's gift to the bride was a princely one, consisting of ten million dollars' worth of the preferred stock of the newly organized American Straw and Hay Trust, of which Colonel Midas was president, a concern controlling all the leading straw industries of the United States and some said of foreign lands as well. The papers called it the most brilliant match of the season, but, none the less, the bride had some misgivings. She knew, and somehow or other in the perspective of the vista of wedded bliss ahead of her, no larger than a pin-head, she seemed at times to see the first faint symptoms of a cloud which might sooner or later obscure the whole heavens; aye, even that vast stretch of blue that reached from the easternmost part of New York to the westernmost boundaries of Reno, Nevada. Still, back of this was a silver — nay, a golden—lining, for Gasmerilda was now the possessor in her own right of five million dollars in real money, and with such a possession in hand one can stand a good deal of domestic misunderstanding.

And even then there was the chance that the sporting instincts of Colonel Midas would prove to be such that he would admire the genius back of the transmutation that had originally won him—in addition to which was the other fact that already, without a bale in sight, he had sold the public over fifty millions' worth of the common stock in the United States Straw and Hay Trust at $97\frac{7}{8}$.

The first check out of Gasmerilda's new account was as follows:

155

JACK AND THE CHECK-BOOK

New York, January 17, 1911
No. 1
Pay to the order of The Fairy's Aid Society
   of America
Seven hundred and fifty thousand Dollars
($750,000.00)
     GASMERILDA MILLER MIDAS

And she lived extravagantly forever afterward.

V

THE INVISIBLE CLOAK

"I AM very sorry, sorr," said the janitor as he turned off the heat and disconnected the electric lights. "'Tain't me as is doin' ut—ut's the owner of the buildin'. He says the rint ain't been paid for six mont's, and while he ain't hard-hearted enough to turn nobody out on the sthreet such weather as this, he don't see no use in dandlin' tinants what don't pay in no lap o' luxury."

Jack looked at the man in silence, completely stunned by this new development in a situation already sufficiently distressing.

157

"'Let him enjye all the pleasures of the roof, Mike,' says he," continued the janitor, "'but no wooin' of his beauty sleep to the soft music of the steam-radiator, nor 'lectric lights to cheer the dark places of his sperrit whin twilight comes. Ut's the land of the Midnight Sun for his till I see th' color of his bank account.'"

"But I shall freeze if you turn off the heat," protested Jack.

"That's the answer, I guess," returned the janitor. "Ut's a pretty cold snap we do be havin'."

Jack buried his face in his hands and groaned. Things had gone ill for the unhappy lad for a long time now, and the sudden precipitation of winter weather found him practically penniless. For one reason or another no one seemed to care for his poetry, and his last story, from the proceeds of which he had expected to make enough to tide him over for a little while at least, had been returned by every editor in town.

THE INVISIBLE CLOAK

"Ut's mighty sorry for you, I am," said the kindly janitor, his heart stirred by the pitiable picture of suffering before him. "I'd be afther leavin' t'ings as they are if I dared, but the old man's orders—"

"I know, I know," said Jack, wearily, "but it's awfully tough just the same. I can get along without food, but without light and heat I don't see how I can do my work."

"I'll lend yez a candle, sorr," said the janitor. "That 'll help some. Ye can warm your hands over the flame of ut while you're doin' your t'inkin', and ut 'll give ye light enough to put down what ye t'ink in between times."

"Good old Mike!" said Jack, wringing the other by the hand warmly. "When my ship comes in you shall have a good slice of the cargo for that."

"Sure an' she ain't la'nched yet, is she?" asked the janitor, with a grin, and then, as Jack seemed to have sunk into a dejected

159

reverie, he gathered up his tools and left the room.

An hour passed before the miserable lad even so much as raised his head.

"Jove! it's cold!" He shivered, as he gazed around him, the room bathed in the gathering shadows of twilight. "And to think that it was only last summer that I was complaining because this place was so infernally hot!"

His teeth chattered as he spoke, and he suddenly bethought himself of his fur-lined overcoat hanging in the closet, his very last possession, and one he had worn persistently of late, not so much because the temperature of the town required it as to maintain publicly an appearance of prosperity.

"I'll take one last wear out of you," he said, as he put it on, "and to-morrow I'll put you in cold storage at the house of mine Uncle. He already has my watch, my scarf-pin, and everything else that I have that is negotiable—he might as well top his collection off with you."

The thought that the useful old garment was still good enough to act as a satisfactory bit of security for a temporary accommodation at the neighboring pawnshop cheered him up somewhat, and he went out, seeking a comfortable spot where with his last half-dollar he could assuage the growing pangs of hunger. As he left the house he noticed that the snow was beginning to fall, so he decided not to go very far afield for his meal. A cheap restaurant half-way down the block, on the avenue, attracted his eye, and he went in and ordered his dinner—twenty-five cents' worth of roast beef and a cup of coffee for himself, and the balance to tip the waiter. He ate slowly, though this was not his habit, merely because the place was warm and bright, and as he lingered over his coffee he wrote a sonnet on life on the back of the bill of fare. Then, his account paid, he started back to his apartment. As he left the café the wheezing notes of a minute hand-organ playing "The Good Old Summer-time" fell upon his ear. It sounded very much like a talking-machine in the last stages of bronchitis, and then, suddenly, in the midst of a "B-flat" that sounded more like a sneeze than a note, a heartrending picture of misery and desolation smote upon his vision. On the corner, exposed to all the icy winds that blew up the avenue, and over the cross-streets from the river, huddled up into a seeming mass of rags, over which the falling snow was drifting, was the form of an aged woman, turning the crank of a battered and broken organ with fitful twists of her poor blue hands.

"Holy smoke!" cried Jack, as his eye fell upon the old woman's bent figure. "And I have been sympathizing with myself for the last four hours!"

In an instant he had whipped off his overcoat—the fur-lined coat that had been his only hope for immediate financial relief—and

162

had thrown it across the poor old shoulders.

"Excuse me, madam," he said, as the old woman stopped grinding the organ to look gratefully up into his face. "If I had any money I'd give it to you, but I'm dead broke myself, and I can't help you that way. But, by thunder! I can't stand seeing you freeze!"

"Oh, I cannot take your coat, sir," the old woman began.

"Yes, you can," said Jack. "If you don't want it as an act of charity, let me have a quarter to buy my breakfast to-morrow morning, and you can have the coat for the time being. I'll rent it to you over-night for a quarter. You can return it in the morning. I live right across the street at the Redmere."

The old woman muttered a scarcely audible word of thanks.

"Heaven will reward you for this," she began.

"That's all right," said Jack, cheerfully.

163

"I'm not looking for dividends of that particular kind. I'll consider it a good bargain if you'll just rent this old horse-blanket for the night for twenty-five cents. Then nobody will be under obligation to anybody else."

The old woman smiled even as she shivered, and diving down into the mysterious depths of her ragged garments produced a handful of pennies which she handed to the unexpected philanthropist.

"I will return the coat in the morning," she said. "Good-night!"

And again the withered hand began to turn the crank, and the suffering organ, as Jack sped across the way to the Redmere again, began to wheeze as before, taking a turn this time at that popular melody, "There'll Be a Hot Time in the Old Town To-night."

"Poor old hag!" muttered Jack as, without removing his clothes, he climbed into bed and covered himself in addition with the

bath-rug. "I may be ninety-seven different kinds of an ass, but here's to the Heart of
Folly! I couldn't let that old creature
freeze to death under my very window."

And warmed by the thought of a kindly
deed done he turned over and went to
sleep.

So weary was the poor lad after the
troublesome experiences of a day so full of
worry that he slept heavily and far into the
next morning. Indeed, it required all the
elbow power of Mike, the janitor, hammering with his great fist upon the door, to
awaken him.

"Hello, there! What the dickens do you
want?" cried Jack, sleepily, aroused at last
from his slumbers by a thunderous kick upon
the door from the janitorial foot.

"Ut's me, sorr," replied Mike.

"Oh, it's you, is it?" said Jack, opening
the door. "What's the trouble now? Orders from the landlord to stop my sleeping?"

"No, sorr," replied the janitor. "Sure

an' I'm just afther bringin' yez a package lift at the door."

"Confound you, Mike!" growled Jack, with a glance at the clock. "Nobody can economize with a noise trust like you around. If you had only let me sleep an hour longer I could have saved the price of a breakfast!"

"Well, the lady that lift this bundle tould me to give ut yez without anny delay," returned Mike. "And whin annybody gives me a dollar to get a move on I get ut."

"A lady gave you a dollar to hand this bundle to me?" demanded Jack, incredulously.

"She did that," said Mike. "She come drivin' up in her limybean motor-car, and give me the package, and tould me not to let anny weeds grow under me slippers."

Jack rubbed his eyes in astonishment, and gazed wonderingly at the brown-paper package. What could it be? Certainly not his fur coat. A limousine car and the lady of the wheezy hand-organ did not seem to go together. In an instant, consumed with curiosity, he tore off the brown-paper covering, and found within a white pasteboard box, oblong in shape, and tied up with blue ribbon. Attached to the middle was a note, which, on being opened, revealed the following message to Jack's staring eyes:

THE UNITED STATES FAIRY COMPANY
8976 WALL STREET

NEW YORK, *December* 12, 1910.

DEAR JACK,—I return your cloak herewith with many thanks for your kindness to

Yours gratefully,

TITANIA J. GODMOTHER,

President The United States Fairy Co.

"Well, I'll be blowed!" ejaculated the lad as he read. "The old lady a fairy? I don't know about this—it has a phony look to me!"

As he spoke he cut the blue ribbon with his penknife and opened the box. The mystery, instead of being solved, now became all the deeper, for as far as Jack's eye was able to see the box was empty.

The janitor grinned unsympathetically.

"Quare toime for an April-fool joke!" he said, as he left the room.

For a few moments Jack was as silent as the Sphinx, and then, with a sudden surge of wrath that any one should play such a trick upon him, he gave the box a kick that sent it flying across the room. It landed on a chair, the cover fell off, and then, mystery of mysteries, three-quarters of the chair disappeared wholly from sight. Again Jack rubbed his eyes in amazement, and slowly, like a trapper passing along a forest trail, he crept over to where the chair stood and put out his hand to feel for its missing parts. In a moment he was reassured as to their existence, for he could feel the outlines of the missing sections, but something apparently lay across them. It was a soft, silky material, tangible enough, but absolutely invisible. It felt like a cloak, and as Jack

"DERE ISS SOMEDINGS IN DOT SEADT, ALRETTY YET!"

passed his hands along its folds he found that it had sleeves, buttons, buttonholes, and a hood at the back of its collar, not to mention several capacious pockets within.

"Huh!" he ejaculated. "It feels like an invisible ulster. I wonder—"

An idea flashed across his mind, acting upon which he seized the cloak, and rushed into his bedroom, where, standing before the mirror on his bureau, he put it on, buttoning it all the way up to his neck. This done, he glanced at himself in the glass.

Only his head, which had remained uncovered, was reflected there!

"Well of all—" he began, astounded at the vision before him, or rather the lack of it. Hastily he pulled the hood over his head, and immediately, as far as the eye could see, he completely vanished.

And then Jack knew what had happened.

The fairy godmother had given him one of the choicest possessions of her kingdom— the famous invisible cloak!

Ten minutes later Jack found himself passing through the Subway gate at Forty-second Street, entirely unobserved by anybody, and therefore relieved of the necessity of paying his fare. The invisible cloak was doing its duty nobly, but a moment later the lad had an example of its dangers as well as of its virtues, for as he sat quietly by the door of the car trying to collect his flustered thoughts, a very stout German gentleman got aboard the train and sat down heavily upon him. He did not stay, however, but on the contrary, with a startled cry of alarm, rose up as quickly as he had sat down.

"Dere iss somedings in dot seadt, alretty yet!" he cried to the guard, excitedly.

Jack slipped noiselessly out of the seat, and the guard, after feeling around in it for a second or two, turned with scorn upon the astonished Teuton, and in language of a slightly unparliamentary cast advised him to change his diet.

"You'll be seein' t'ings next!" he said.

THE INVISIBLE CLOAK

Jack shook with internal laughter as the amazed son of the Rhine sat cautiously down again, his face showing a deal of relief to find that his first spooky impression was not correct, all of which for the remainder of the trip down-town he openly expressed with considerable volubility. Finally he was interrupted by the raucous voice of the guard crying:

"Wall Street!"

Now Jack had not consciously started out to go to Wall Street, but the announcement of the train's arrival there gave him a thrill.

"Wall Street, eh?" he muttered. "Ha! Hum! Methinks the financial stringency is over if this little old coat holds out! I seem to detect the odor of money."

He mounted the steps to the street, and wandered aimlessly down the great financial highway until he found himself standing before the gorgeous façade of the famous Urban National Bank. Here he paused a moment, and curiosity as much as anything else led him to enter its portals, and there within lay spread before his famished financial eyes, separated from his hands only by a slight bit of steel grillwork, countless packages, huge of bulk, of bank-notes, in all denominations, any one of which, once in his possession, would serve to put him at ease for the remainder of the year. Monte Cristo himself had no such stores of wealth within his reach in the treasure-caves of his wondrous island. The teller behind the grill was counting the contents of his safe, and as he bent over to foot up a column of figures Jack stopped in front of the little window and said:

"Good-morning!"

He did this not so much for the fun of it as for a precautionary test of his invisibility, for a great scheme had entered his mind. The teller looked up, craned his neck in every direction, and peered around to see who had addressed him.

"There must be something the matter

"THERE MUST BE SOMETHING THE MATTER WITH
MY NERVES"

with my nerves this morning," he said, scratching his head in bewilderment. "I was sure somebody spoke to me."

Jack had all he could do to keep from laughing outright, but safety bade him restrain the impulse, and in a moment he had climbed over the steel grillwork and entered the sacred precincts of Ready Money. Once within the teller's cage his heart began to thump so violently that it seemed impossible for him to escape detection, but so busy were all the bank people with the duties of the day that no one seemed to hear. And then our hero began. Within five minutes he had stowed away within the capacious pockets of his invisible cloak as many of the packages of bills, green-backed and yellow, as he could possibly carry there, and then, slipping out through the little door at the rear of the cage, he walked calmly out of the bank with them. Arrived on Broadway, he removed his coat and, hanging it over his arm, took a taxicab back to the Redmere.

He could hardly wait until he reached his apartment to count up the results of his morning's work, but his caution stood by him, and it was not until he had locked his door and barricaded it with the bureau rolled in front of it that he opened the various packages. There were ten of them altogether, and Jack's eyes nearly popped out of his head with wonder as he saw so much real money spread out before him. Three of the packages held one thousand dollars each in twenty-dollar bills, four of them held five hundred dollars each in five-dollar bills, and the other three totalled fifteen hundred dollars in ones and twos—sixty-five hundred dollars altogether.

"Mike!" he cried, going to the dumbwaiter shaft, and calling down, vociferously, "turn on the heat, and tell the boss to send a truck around here for his rent."

Hiding the money under the mattress of his bed, Jack removed the invisible cloak and hung it in the closet, taking care to lock the door thereof, and then he started to shave. His hand trembled too much for this, however, and after he had snipped off two or three pieces of his cheek he abandoned the effort, but his brief trial before the glass had a distinct moral influence upon him, for as his eye caught its own reflection in the mirror, and Jack came to look himself squarely in the face for the first time since his removal of the money from the bank, he found that he could not do it. His eye faltered and fell, and the question flashed across his mind as to the honesty of his morning's work.

"Hum!" he muttered, sitting down suddenly on his bed and staring at a hole in the carpet, "I hadn't thought of that before! What would my poor but honest parents think about this?"

He scratched the end of his nose thoughtfully.

"It isn't any too straight, even in these days of frenzied finance," he went on; "that is, it isn't unless I regard this thing as a loan! Of course if it's a loan—yes, it must be. Otherwise I'm no better than any other—"

His brow cleared as the idea entered his mind.

"I'll make it O. K. in a jiffy," he said.

He went to his writing-desk, and wrote to the cashier of the Urban National Bank as follows:

New York, *December* 12, 1910.
Cashier, the Urban National Bank,
New York City;

Dear Sir,—I think it only proper to inform you that, unknown to yourself or any other person in your bank, I have this morning negotiated a loan with your institution for six thousand five hundred dollars. I have a temporary need for this accommodation, and in order that the transaction may appear a trifle less informal, I beg to hand you herewith my six-months note for the amount borrowed, together with one hundred and ninety-five dollars in cash to cover discount charges, reckoned on a six-per-cent. basis. Please acknowledge receipt of the same in the Personal Column of the New York *Morning Gazoo.*

The charming ease and promptness with which

this transaction was put through have given me a
more than friendly feeling for your bank, and now
that I have used one package of your money I
take pleasure in saying that I shall not only recom-
mend it to my friends, but shall hereafter use no
other.

Cordially yours,
A FRIEND IN NEED.

This written, Jack purchased a blank
promissory note at a stationery store on the
corner and filled it in.

> $6,500.   NEW YORK, *December* 12, 1910.
> Six months after date I promise to pay to
> the order of the Urban National Bank Six
> thousand five hundred dollars at the Urban
> National Bank, New York City.
> Value received.   ME.

Both these interesting documents he now
inclosed in an envelope, with one hundred
and ninety-five dollars in bills, sending the
whole by special-delivery mail to the
cashier of the bank.

"There!" said Jack, when he had completed this righteous act. "I can now look myself in the eye again."

From this time on Jack wore his invisible cloak nearly all the time. He found it very convenient, especially when he wished to go to the theatre, or to ride on any of our vehicles of public transportation. Once he seriously contemplated a trip to Europe in it, but this was postponed by a sudden important development which called for his attention nearer home. While seated in the back of Colonel Midas's box at the Metropolitan Opera House one night, listening to the dreamy numbers of "La Bohème," utterly unobserved, of course, by any of the other occupants of the box, thanks to his magic cloak, Jack overheard Colonel Midas engaged in a strenuous conversation with one of his male relatives, who had asked the eminent financier for some kind of a tip that would make a rich man of him.

"If you'll tell me whether the San Fran-

cisco, Omaha & Mott Haven is going to
buy the K., T. & W. or not, Colonel," the
man had said, "I can make a million or
two."

"Of course you could, Jim," said the
Colonel, "but I can't tell you now what will
be done in that matter. I don't know myself whether we'll buy K., T. & W. or build
our own connecting line. We haven't decided. If we do buy, the stock will go jumping up ten, twenty, thirty points at a time.
If we don't, the bottom will drop out of it.
It's the turn of a hand which way that cat
will jump, but I'll do this for you: As soon
as I do know I'll give you twenty-four hours'
start with the inside information. We have
a secret meeting to-morrow at my office to
discuss the matter, and when we come to a
definite understanding I'll give you the tip.
What I can tell you now is that the new line
into Buffalo is going to run through Rocky
Corners, and anybody who gets hold of old
Hiram Bumpus's farm up there under a

hundred thousand will clear half a million without getting out of bed."

"Why don't you go in and buy it yourself?" demanded the other.

"Because I'm not wasting my gray matter on piking little half-million-dollar deals, that's why," retorted Midas, with a glance of scorn at his guest.

Bursting with this valuable information, Jack immediately left the Opera House and dispatched a rush telegram to Hiram Bumpus at Rocky Corners offering him fifty thousand dollars for his farm.

The answer came back the next morning:

Price of farm seventy-five thousand, cash. No checks taken. HIRAM BUMPUS.

To which Jack immediately replied: "Price satisfactory. Will arrive Thursday with money."

This done, our hero proceeded to camp on the front doorstep of Colonel Midas, and when that distinguished financier appeared to take his motor down to his office Jack, still wearing his invisible cloak, climbed in alongside of him, and hardly daring to breathe lest he should betray his presence in the car, rode down to the offices of the Midas Trust Company with the magnate himself. Here Midas descended from the car, and Jack, close upon his heels, followed him into that holy of financial holies, the private office.

"Any word from Rockernegie?" asked the Colonel of his secretary, as he seated himself at his desk, Jack meanwhile having perched himself on the mantelpiece.

"Here at ten," returned the secretary, laconically. They did not even waste breath in that office.

"Moneypenny?"

"Wires, here ten-fifteen."

"Asterbilt?"

"Yachting. Mediterranean. Leaves all to you."

"Good!" said Midas. "When they come

185

show them in, and I'm out to everybody else."

And then it was that Jack had his first glimpse of really great men in action. By ten-thirty all the magnates of finance, with the exception of Mr. Asterbilt, were on hand, and the secret meeting of the rulers of the San Francisco, Omaha & Mott Haven Transcontinental Railway System was on. They came down to business without any preliminaries.

"Is it buy or build?" asked Midas.

"Buy," said Rockernegie.

"Build," said Moneypenny.

"All right—we buy," said Midas.

"It's a hold-up," said Moneypenny. "K., T. & W. was built for no other purpose."

"Perfectly true," said Midas. "Therefore, instead of announcing that we shall buy, thus sending the price up till it bumps against the Dipper, let us announce that we have decided to build our own connecting line, and when K., T. & W. lands down around 1⅛ we can go in and scoop it."

"Always right, Midas," said Rocker-negie.

"I'll change my vote and make it unanimous," said Moneypenny, whereupon the Colonel passed the cigars and the meeting stood adjourned. It had taken seven minutes to settle a question involving millions upon millions of dollars, and for a moment Jack stood aghast, but for no longer than a moment, for the time for him to get busy had arrived. He was in possession of the most valuable secret on Wall Street, and it behooved him to begin operations. Passing hastily out of the office, he first paid a visit to the Urban National, where after an hour's hard work he succeeded in getting $300,000 out of the vaults, leaving on the cashier's desk, while he was out at lunch, as security for his loan, a sufficient amount of gilt-edged collateral, also taken from the vaults of the bank itself.

"It's all right," Jack wrote in his memorandum to the cashier. "I have a big transaction on hand which can't help win out, and I shall rejoice your heart by liquidating all my loans with you before spring. After all, my dear sir, all business must be done on confidence, and I assure you you can have plenty in me. I know myself through and through, and can testify to my absolute integrity. Meanwhile let me repeat that your money is the best I have ever used, and is received everywhere with real enthusiasm."

That night before he retired, operating through a dozen brokers' offices so as not to attract undue attention, Jack purchased five thousand shares of K., T. & W. at 20, paying for them in cash. The next morning on the announcement from Colonel Midas's office that the San Francisco, Omaha & Mott Haven road had decided not to take over the property, K., T. & W. fell off to 10, at which figure, after a hurried visit to the bank, Jack acquired ten thousand more shares. At the end of the week K., T. & W. had slumped to 3⅛, whereat Jack pyramided by taking over twenty thousand more, all paid for in cash, having meanwhile sent his lawyer to Rocky Corners with seventy-five thousand dollars to close his real-estate deal with Hiram Bumpus.

In the brief period of ten days the unfortunate tenant of the freezing apartment at the Redmere had become the owner of fifty thousand shares of K., T. & W., as well as the proprietor of a thirty-thousand-acre farm through which a new line of railway was sure to pass.

So the campaign went on over the Christmas season. Jack, by following close on the heels of Midas or Moneypenny, it mattered little which, secured inside information as to every deal of magnitude on Wall Street whole days, and even weeks, before anybody else knew about it; and having the resources of the Urban National to draw upon at need, he was never at a loss how to finance himself. January came, and just as it seemed as if K., T. & W. was about to be wiped out of existence came the report that the property had been acquired by the San Francisco, Omaha & Mott Haven crowd, and that its stock had been put on an eight-per-cent. guaranteed-dividend basis. The quotation immediately began to soar. K., T. & W. began to jump like a kangaroo. First it leaped to 30, then to 68. On the tenth of January it opened at 128⅜, and closed at 150, where it stuck. For a time Jack waited for a further rise, but it failed to come, and in February he sold one hundred and twenty thousand shares, which had cost him on an average of $7 a share, for $150 a share, realizing a profit of $17,160,000. Reference to his books showed that he had drawn on the Urban National for a trifle over $1,250,-000, which sum he now started to return in the same laborious fashion in which it had been acquired. Every day for a period of ten days the lad would put on his invisible cloak, and at the cashier's lunch-hour would walk into his office and deposit a great bundle of currency on his desk. Once he found that gentleman, and the president of the bank as well, awaiting him, but it made no difference. Secure in the concealment of his marvellous cloak, Jack stood in the doorway and tossed the package of bills into the room, hitting the astonished president of the bank himself squarely in the stomach with it.

In this way complete restitution with interest was made, and on the first of February Jack found himself clear of all obligations, with a comfortable fortune of over \$15,000,000 on his hands, which made any further involuntary loans on the bank's part unnecessary; but what was even better than this, the meteoric successes of the young millionaire upon the Street brought him such renown that it was not long before the powers began to take notice.

"That young man," said Colonel Midas, after watching him for a little while, "is the most singularly astute person I ever met. I don't wish to be vulgar, but he has been the nigger in every woodpile I have tackled for six months. He knows what I am going to do almost as quick as I do. We'll have to take him in the firm."

"He has a singularly keen premonition as to values," observed Mr. Rockernegie. "I've half a mind to start a trust company and make him president."

As for Mr. Moneypenny, after a year's experience at finding Jack at the bottom of pretty nearly every scheme he went into, he made the following observation to his daughter, as he pointed Jack out to her at the opera—in his own box now—one night.

"That young man in the third box on the left, my dear, is young Mr. Jack Hardluck. He's so keen that I don't even dare think what I'm going to do for fear he'll find it out!"

"If that's the case, papa," said Miss Moneypenny, blushing, "the best thing to do is to take him into the family. Don't you think you'd better—"

The girl hung her head shyly.

"Better what, my dear?" asked the old billionaire, kindly.

"Give him to me for a Christmas present?" she answered. "I think I could get to like him very, very much."

And, indeed, that is how it came to be that in due course of time the young financier became the son-in-law of one of the financial powers of the world.

As for the invisible cloak, Jack wears it now only to travel *incog.*, which for a multi-millionaire is sometimes convenient.

Incidentally and in conclusion, let me add that Mike Brannigan, once the janitor of the Redmere, is now the owner of that handsome apartment - house, having received the title - deeds through the mails from some anonymous benefactor.

"Who the divvle sint it, I dinnaw!" he said. "Nor what for he done it, nayther. I ain't never done nothin' to injure nobody!"

VI

THE RETURN OF ALADDIN

IGHT had fallen over the city, but the work in the little tailor shop on the Bowery still went on. The toiling widow of Mustafa, the incorporated valet of the Bachelors' Aid Society, who had died the winter before, leaving his family with nothing but a few debts and his ironing-board, was wearily struggling with the last batch of undarned socks received that morning from the association. She sighed deeply as she labored, for her fingers were sore with many stitches.

"Heigho!" she murmured, sadly. "Why

don't these bachelors get married and have this sort of thing done at home, I wonder? This is the ten-thousandth sock I have darned since Christmas, and as for the suspender buttons, the good Lord only knows how many of those I have sewed on. There ought to be a law compelling men to marry on penalty of having to do their own mending."

Poor woman! In the weariness of her spirit she little dreamed that she was growing petulant with her bread and butter. Suddenly she heard the door of the little shop without open, and her son Aladdin entered, a great, buoyant lad of twenty, cheerful of spirit and a good deal of a giant physically.

"Well, Worthless," she said, with an affectionate glance into his fine eyes, "where have you been all day?"

"Looking for work, mother, as usual," said the young man, throwing a small package on the table. "And you?"

"The same old drudgery, dear," she replied, with a sigh. "Did you have any luck?"

"No, mother dear, not a bit," replied Aladdin.

"Do you mean to tell me that in all this great city there is no work of any kind that a hale, hearty, hungry boy like you can get to do?" she demanded.

"Plenty of it, mother," replied the boy; "plenty of it, but nothing in my special line. Lots of snow-shovelling jobs and a position as guard on the Subway were offered me, but I cannot demean myself by taking anything of that sort, Mummsy dear. Father in the last days of his life spent too many hours teaching me how to raise mushrooms under glass for me to dishonor his memory by undertaking labor that is beneath that in artistic quality, and just at present I cannot find anybody in all this city who wants a helper in mushroom culture."

"Then we shall have to go supperless to

bed," sighed the poor woman. "Not a penny in the house and the pantry bare. Oh, Aladdin, Aladdin, why will you not give up this false pride of yours and get some kind of a job that will at least feed yourself and help me pay the rent?"

The boy was silent. He had had this same argument with his mother time and time and again, and he was quite aware of the futility of speech in trying to overcome her objections to what she termed his incorrigible idleness.

"What have you in the package?" the woman asked, after a prolonged silence.

"I don't know," replied Aladdin. "I picked it up outside the stage-door of the Helicon Theatre. I saw it lying in the snow and I brought it along with me. It is probably some kind of a make-up box belonging to one of the performers. If there is any reward offered in any of the morning papers for its return, maybe I shall earn a few honest pennies by taking it back to its owner."

"HUMPH!" SAID SHE, SCORNFULLY

THE RETURN OF ALADDIN

His mother busied herself with the string, and in a moment it came untied and a small brass lamp rolled out of the brown-paper covering. It was very dirty and much battered.

"Humph!" said she, scornfully, gazing at the homely little object. "I don't think anybody will be foolish enough to offer a reward for a trumpery little thing like that."

"Ah, well," said Aladdin, gazing out of the shop window at the scurrying crowds on the sidewalk, "it might be worse, Mummsy dear. We at least have a roof over our heads this night, which is more than some of those poor wretches have, and unless I am very much mistaken this storm that is upon us is going to be a blizzard."

In very truth a blizzard had descended upon the city. All the transportation lines were blocked, and over on Broadway all traffic had been tied up for hours. Thanks to the elevated-railway structure, this portion of the Bowery still remained passable.

201

Even this was momentarily piling higher and higher with the snow, and the wind was in one of its most violently rampageous moods.

"How would you feel if your little Aladdin had a job as a chauffeur on a night like this?" the lad went on.

The poor woman shuddered and was about to reply, when a terrific crash from without drove all thought of words from her mind. Hastily running to the window, she, too, peered out into the street for a moment over Aladdin's shoulder, but only for a moment, for in an instant the boy was up and making for the door of the little tailor shop. A heavy limousine car lay overturned upon its side upon the walk, its wheels having skidded on the slippery, snow-covered pavement, and striking the curb, toppled completely over. Aladdin, with the agility of a small monkey, soon mounted to the upper side of the overturned vehicle, and, opening the door, had assisted a beautifully arrayed young woman, possibly a year or two younger than himself, from within, and after her, fuming and condemning his luck and the world in general, a gray-haired and apparently irascible old gentleman.

"Mother!" cried Aladdin, as the girl fainted in his arms, "come quickly. The young lady has fainted."

The good woman needed no second bidding. She hastened to his side, and the limp form of the young girl was carried in her strong, motherly arms into the little back room behind the tailor shop, which formed their only home. Shortly afterward the old gentleman came also, ushered in by Aladdin.

"She is safe?" cried he, with an anxious glance at the prostrate form of his daughter.

"Perfectly so, sir," replied Aladdin's mother. "She has only fainted. Won't you sit down, sir?" she added. "You look a little shaken up yourself."

"Thank you," said the old gentleman, gazing around the room vainly in search of a chair. "Ah—what shall I sit down on, madam?"

"Try the stove, sir," laughed Aladdin. "It may warm it up a bit."

The old man gazed frowningly at the boy, not relishing such levity at so serious a moment, and Aladdin, slightly embarrassed by his own frivolity, tried to cover his confusion by seizing the lamp that had fallen from the package, and polishing its highly oxidized surface by rubbing it on the patched knee of his trousers. And then a strange thing came to pass. At the moment of the first attrition between his knee and the little brass lamp the room seemed to fill with a gray mist and in its gathering depths Aladdin perceived the huge figure of a blackamoor gradually taking shape.

"What the dickens!" muttered the lad to himself as the strange apparition rose up before him, rubbing his eyes to make sure that he saw clearly. "What do you want?"

he added, springing to his feet as the genie approached him.

"I have come in response to your summons," replied the blackamoor. "Give your orders, sir!"

Aladdin grinned broadly at this. The idea of his ever giving orders to anybody seemed so very absurd. Nevertheless, he fell in with the spirit of the hour.

"All right, Sambo," he returned. "Get this gentleman a chair. There may be an extra one up-stairs in the music-room."

The blackamoor disappeared for an instant and shortly returned bringing with him the desired piece of furniture.

"Thank you," said the old gentleman, as he took his seat with an uneasy glance around him. The situation was not altogether without alarming features. As for Aladdin, you could have knocked him over with a palm-leaf fan, so astonished was he at this unusual development.

"I wish I'd asked for something to eat," he muttered to himself.

"So do I," observed the old gentleman. "I'd give five hundred dollars just now for a boiled egg."

"You ought to get one studded with diamonds at that price," laughed Aladdin, and then just for a joke he turned to the blackamoor. "Get this gentleman five hundred dollars' worth of boiled eggs, Sambo," he said.

"Hard or soft, sir?" asked the genie.

"Three minutes," said the old gentleman.

Sambo made a low salaam to Aladdin, and departing, he returned four minutes later followed by seven other blackamoors just like him, each carrying a large wicker hamper on his shoulders. These they deposited in various parts of the room, and, gravely opening them, disclosed to the astounded gaze of Aladdin and his unknown guest hundreds of eggs, steaming as though freshly taken from the pot,

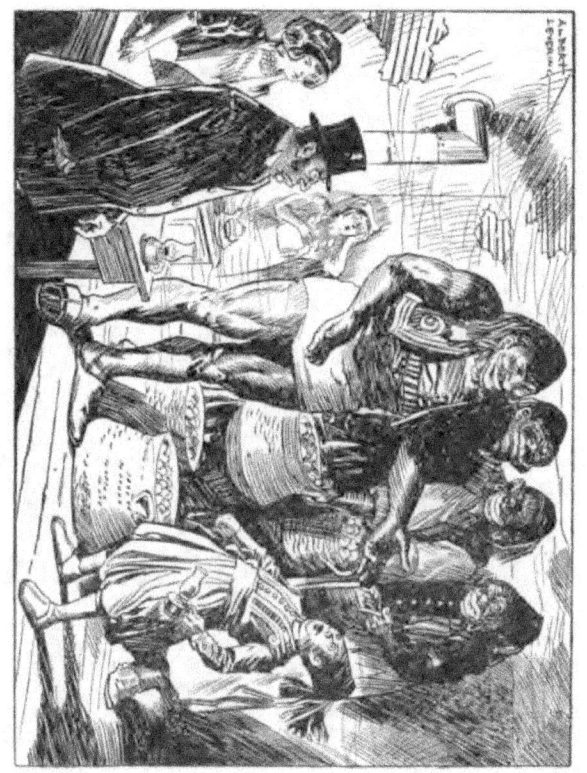

"THIS IS A HALF-PORTION, SIR," SAID SAMBO

"This is a half-portion, sir," said Sambo, addressing Aladdin. "We will return with the remainder in a minute, sir."

"Just wait a second," said Aladdin, scratching his head in bewilderment at the sight of so many eggs obtained with such ease. "It may be that these will be enough for the time being. I'll ask the old chap. Excuse me, Mr.—er—Mr.—er, I didn't catch your name, sir."

"I am Major Bondifeller, president of the United Mints of North America," replied the old gentleman. "A person not to be trifled with, young man, as you probably know very well."

Aladdin gasped, as well he might. Here was old Rufus Bondifeller, reputed to be the richest man in the world, a guest in his mother's fast-failing little remnant of a tailor shop.

"Gud-glad to mum-meet you, sir," stammered Aladdin. "Do you think there's enough eggs here to satisfy your hunger?

There appears to be two hundred and fifty dollars' worth here now, but if you wish the rest served immediately—"

"Great heavens, no!" roared Bondifeller. "When I said I'd give five hundred dollars for a boiled egg I was merely speaking figuratively. A rich man can't eat any more boiled eggs at a sitting than a poor man; fact is, half the time he can't eat as many without a bad attack of angina pectoris."

"All right," said Aladdin, resolved to carry off the extraordinary situation with an outward nonchalance, in spite of the inner turmoil that kept his brain whirling. "You needn't bother about the rest of those eggs now, Sambo. Major Bondifeller can get along on these."

The blackamoor and his companions disappeared even as they had come, apparently irrespective of doorways, and utterly regardless of walls. They seemed merely to melt through whatever solid substances there might be between themselves and annihilation. As for Major Bondifeller, as he observed these strange developments, his face grew set and rigid. He eyed every movement of the blackamoors with uneasy attention until they had vanished from sight, and then his flashing eye was riveted upon Aladdin. Finally he spoke, sharply and to the point.

"Well," he snapped, "how much?"

Aladdin started. The icy tone of the speaker's voice chilled him, and it was so peremptory that he felt for the moment as if he had been stung by the lash.

"How much what?" he said, finally, summoning up all his courage to face the apparently angry millionaire.

"Don't try to evade the point," retorted the Major, coldly. "Let's get through with the business as quickly as we can. It is plain as a pikestaff to anybody having half an eye that, taking advantage of our mishap, you have lured my daughter and myself in here for your own profit. No man keeps such a villainous-looking gang of niggers on hand with an honest purpose. So what are your demands?"

Aladdin laughed in spite of his disturbed frame of mind at the Major's suspicions. It was such an absurd idea that he could be at the head of a badger-gang, and yet, after all, he could not deny a certain sort of reasonableness in the notion from Major Bondifeller's point of view. Again taking the lamp casually in his hand, more as an outlet for his embarrassment than for any other reason, he gave it a second rub and started to answer the Major's question, but, as before, the mist again appeared, and from its musty depths the blackamoor took shape and salaamed before him.

"Well, what is it now, Sambo?" demanded Aladdin, frowning at the intruder.

"Your orders, sir," said the blackamoor. "You rubbed the lamp, I believe?"

Aladdin's heart leaped into his mouth. *He had rubbed the lamp twice, and twice had*

"YOU RUBBED THE LAMP, I BELIEVE?"

it brought him aid! Surely, there must be some magic about this.

"What if I did rub the lamp?" he queried, in a tremulous voice. "What's that got to do with you?"

"I and my comrades are slaves of the lamp, as your Highness very well knows," replied the blackamoor. "Whatever your commands, the United Order of Amalgamated Genii must obey."

"*Hooray!*" cried Aladdin, dancing a wild fandango about the room. "*Who wants the handsome waiter?*"

As the full import of his new-found treasure dawned upon his mind, the lad's ecstasy bade fair to surpass all bounds, but the chilling voice of Bondifeller served to calm his effervescing spirit.

"I want nothing but your proposition, so that I may get out of this den as speedily as possible," he was saying. "I am not a man to beat about the bush, and I realize that you have got me. What is it you demand?"

JACK AND THE CHECK-BOOK

"First and foremost, civility," said Aladdin, boldly, a sense of his own power sweeping over him and giving him confidence.
"I guess you'll find that harder to negotiate
than a check for a considerable sum, Major
Bondifeller, cash being a commoner com-
modity with you than civility. Now, as a
matter of fact, sir," the lad went on, "I had
your daughter carried in here out of that
raging blizzard so that my mother could
give her the attention she needed. You I
brought in also with no more knowledge of
who you were, and with no more idea of
financially profiting by your accident, than
if you had been one of those unfortunate
tramps out on the Bowery there. But now
that you have put the idea in my mind that,
perhaps, after all, nobody ever does anything unselfishly in this world, I will make
certain demands of you. To begin with,
you may pay me two hundred and fifty dollars for those eggs, and as a mere act of
ordinary generosity, you may tip the hand-
216

some waiter fifty dollars. I understand, too, sir, that you are the proprietor of these ten city blocks in which I and about twenty thousand of my neighbors are housed?"

"I believe I do own considerable property hereabouts," said the millionaire, sullenly, "though I can't say offhand whether I do or not. My agents look after my smaller investments."

"Well," said Aladdin, "it don't make any difference to me whether you remember what you own or not. The results so far as you are concerned will be the same. You will have these ten blocks of houses torn down and replaced by model tenements, turning the alternate blocks into city parks for the children to play in."

"But suppose I don't own 'em?" protested Bondifeller.

"What you don't own, Major Bondifeller," returned Aladdin, "is too trifling a detail for us to worry over. So long as you don't own me I don't care a pickled herring

217

what you do own. If it turns out upon investigation that any of these pig-pens on these ten city squares belong to anybody else, buy 'em."

"Buy 'em?" snarled Bondifeller. "How can I buy 'em if the other man won't sell?"

"With money," said Aladdin; "the same stuff you always use to buy anything else you happen to want, from an oil-painting or a Japanese porcelain up to a State legislature or a man's conscience."

"And if I don't agree?" demanded the old man, a truculent glare in his eye, an eye before which the so-called powerful men of the earth had trembled more than once in the past.

Aladdin returned the gaze unflinchingly. Once more he rubbed the lamp, and the genie appeared as before.

"Sambo," said the lad, calmly, with a wink at the slave, "is dungeon number thirty-seven on the fifteenth tier below the Subway occupied to-night?"

"No, sir," replied the blackamoor, with a grin.

"Very well, then," said Aladdin, coldly; "you may provide a special escort of fifteen of your best and most reliable genii and have them take this young lady to her home at Zoocrest, Central Park East, taking care that nothing shall occur either to frighten her or to make her uncomfortable in any way. Meanwhile, you yourself, with five of our biggest huskies, will file this gentleman here away for the night in dungeon number thirty-seven, as aforesaid."

"As your Highness directs," replied the obedient blackamoor.

In a moment the still prostrate form of Miss Bondifeller was borne gently from the room and placed in a large touring-car that suddenly materialized without, and shortly Bondifeller, sitting ruefully alone in the little back room, could hear it chugging up the snowbound street at as lively a pace as any racer ever struck upon the smoothest of boulevards. It was indeed an illuminating exhibition of the remarkable resources of this extraordinary young man, and, strange to say, a contemplation of it gave the old gentleman a curious sense of pleasure. To be sure, he appeared to be in rather a bad predicament, but all the same it was a novel sensation to him to encounter somebody who apparently did not fear him. This was an emotion that he had not enjoyed for many years, and it was not without its titillation.

"I guess you've got me, young man," he said, rather meekly, when Aladdin returned.

"I guess that's a good guess," retorted Aladdin, nonchalantly. "There's only one answer to the question that confronts you, and you've lit on it the very first time. I don't intend to be at all vindictive, Major Bondifeller," he continued, "but a little lesson in arbitrary power isn't going to do you a bit of harm; so just make up your mind to take your medicine, and let's save our breath to talk of more important things.

First thing, I'm hungry. Mother, please lay covers for three—"

"But, my son," began the poor woman, who, in caring for the unconscious girl, had seen nothing of what was going on, "we haven't a morsel of food in the—"

"Do as I say, mother," said Aladdin, quickly. "Sambo will attend to the rest."

"Gone clean out of his head, poor laddy!" murmured his mother, hastening, nevertheless, to fulfil his commands, merely as a means of keeping him quiet. Meanwhile, Aladdin, seizing the faithful lamp, gave it another rub, and when the blackamoor appeared he ordered a royal repast—so royal, indeed, that old Major Bondifeller's eyes nearly popped out of his head as he ran over the order. A few suppers of that sort would have bankrupted even so flourishing a concern as the United Mints of North America.

"Any favorite dish you'd like to add, Major?" asked Aladdin, genially.

The old man's eyes filled with tears at this

exhibition of kindness, even at this moment when they were practically enemies at swords' points. He could not remember in his own line of effort in many years that he had himself ever extended any consideration to a fallen foe.

"Why, I don't know," said he, his voice growing husky with emotion. "Sometimes in the midst of all the luxury I am enjoying to-day my mind runs back to those early days on the old farm when my mother's apple pies seemed to be the perfection of culinary art."

"Say no more, Major; you shall have your wish," laughed Aladdin. Then, turning to the waiting attendant, he added, "Sambo, you may add to that order one full portion of pallid pippin pie for pale people, with a glass of buttermilk on the side."

An hour later the happy little party—for Major Bondifeller had warmed up considerably under the exhilarating influence of his strange surroundings—broke up with a sense of repletion that neither Aladdin nor his poor mother had enjoyed for many years. Indeed, it is doubtful if the young man himself had ever had so square a meal as that in all his life before. Over the cigars, Bondifeller tried to take up the thread of their before-dinner discourse.

"As for that business suggestion of yours—" he began, flicking the ash airily from the end of his cigar, but Aladdin stopped him.

"I make it a rule never to talk business at or immediately after dinner, Major," he said, reprovingly. "The hour is late and dungeon number thirty-seven awaits you. I trust you will sleep well. Sambo, show this gentleman to his room."

"But—" began Bondifeller.

"On your way, Sambo!" said Aladdin. "And, remember, that if this gentleman turns up missing in the morning you lose your union card. Good-night!"

When Aladdin awoke the following morning it was only natural that he should regard the events of the night before as nothing more than a fantastic dream, and he was chuckling softly to himself over its manifest absurdities, when all of a sudden he spied the lamp on the table of his humble little room. He eyed it keenly for a few minutes, and then springing from the bed he seized it in his left hand and began rubbing it feverishly with his right. As had invariably happened before, the genie responded on the instant.

"Your orders, your Highness," he said.

Aladdin scratched his head in sheer bewilderment, but, pulling himself together by a strong effort of will, he answered, somewhat haughtily:

"Send a maid to my mother's room immediately with instructions to replenish her wardrobe at once with whatever things she may choose to ask for, and you may yourself bring me my new frock coat, with the lavender trousers and the white piqué vest.

You may lay out my best shirred-front shirt and my mauve tie, and see that my silk socks match the latter. I shall wear my patent-leather shoes this morning, and if my silk hat shows any signs of wear, get me a new one."

"Yes, your Highness," said the blackamoor. "And will your Grace breakfast?"

"Yes," said Aladdin. "Have breakfast on the table in one hour from now—fried eggs, buckwheat cakes, tenderloin steak, and a little salt fish. I desire, also, to have Major Bondifeller at breakfast with me, and, mind you, tell him not to keep me waiting."

"As your Highness wills," said the blackamoor, retiring.

Aladdin's orders were fulfilled to the letter, and after the breakfast was over he summoned the genie with a considerable flourish, which deeply impressed his guest.

"Now, Sambo," said he, "I want you to take the limousine, go up to the St. Gotham Hotel and inform the proprietor that Monsieur Le Duc di Lumière will arrive there, with his mother the Countess de Bougie, and suite, precisely at noon, and desires the best accommodations the house can provide. To inspire confidence you would better take a few diamond necklaces with you and deposit them for safe-keeping at the office; and while you are about it, I'd like a couple of thousand dollars for pocket-money."

As he gave these orders Aladdin scarcely dared look at the genie, for fear of rebellion, but they seemed to make no impression at all upon the blackamoor, who merely bowed his acquiescence and handed Aladdin a bag full of gold pieces. As for the Major, who had passed a sleepless night, he merely blinked amazedly at these astounding occurrences. Finally, he found his voice. "You are the Duc di Lumière?" he asked.

"At your service," said Aladdin.

"And may I ask what you are doing here in these squalid quarters?" continued the old man.

"I am conducting a personal investigation into the lives of the unfortunate," replied Aladdin. "By some extraordinary good chance the Fates have thrown you, who are largely responsible for the awful conditions I find here, intó my hands, with power to control your movements. Within a radius of ten city blocks, Major Bondifeller, there are enough human souls living in squalid misery to populate a New England city, and yet you pay no more attention to them, nay, not as much, as you pay to a fly that enters your house and buzzes around your pate. You give the fly some personal attention, but in this matter of your tenements you do nothing whatsoever, leaving it to an agent to care for your smaller interests. I believe those are your own words. Now, sir, it is in my power to keep you here for as long a time as I wish, but I don't want to make a prisoner of you. I want to give you a chance to do something for your fellow - men, especially those who can never hope to repay you save in gratitude. You heard my views last' night. I ask nothing for myself, for, as you see, I do not need anything for myself. I have but to order what I wish, and it is here."

"Your model tenements are a useless ideal," retorted Bondifeller. "Only last year, at enormous expense, I put bath-tubs in all my tenements, and my agent reports that the tenants use them to store their coal in."

"And do you know why?" demanded Aladdin.

"Ignorance, I presume," said Bondifeller, "allied to a love of squalor."

"Nothing of the sort!" retorted Aladdin, pounding the table with his fist. "It is because you spent all your appropriation on bath-tubs and never even thought of putting one penny into the construction of coal-bins."

Bondifeller was silent. He had never thought of that before.

"Well," he said, ruefully, "I suppose I must agree, but it will cost twenty millions of dollars."

"What's twenty millions to a man who controls the United Mints of North America?" demanded Aladdin.

"But if you keep me here I shall not control the United Mints of North America!" shouted Bondifeller, pounding the table just a little on his own account. "John W. Midas and Silas Reddymun have combined against me, and if I am not at the board meeting at ten o'clock this morning I am down and out."

"Phew!" whistled Aladdin. "By Jove! Major, I'm glad you mentioned it in time. It gives me an opportunity to show you just what this power of mine amounts to."

He rubbed the lamp and the genie appeared.

"I desire the immediate presence here of Colonel John W. Midas and Mr. Silas Reddymun, Sambo," said Aladdin.

229

"To hear is to obey," replied the slave, making off.

"You don't mean to say—" gasped Bondifeller.

"Major Bondifeller," said Aladdin, "I am not the saying kind. I am a plain, common garden doer. I admit that this time I am stretching things a point, but you'll find my orders are obeyed."

As indeed they were, to the astonishment of all concerned, not even excepting Aladdin himself, who trembled at the audacity of his last command. Within forty minutes the two gasping financiers whose presence had been commanded sat before them. The genii had apparently taken them just as they found them, for Reddymun still wore his bath-robe and Midas was in his shirt-sleeves, with only one side of his face shaved.

"What the devil does this mean?" they demanded, in scarcely varying terms.

"It means," said Aladdin, calmly, now very sure of himself—as he had every right

" WHAT DOES THIS MEAN ?" THEY DEMANDED

to be, considering the already successful manifestation of his powers—"it means, gentlemen, that the United Mints of North America have passed into the control of a dark horse, who is familiarly known to himself as Aladdin, Duc di Lumière, and that unless you magnates get together inside of one hour and do something to clean up the squalor and misery of this city as represented by these cesspools of humanity termed the tenement districts, you will spend the balance of your days in something worse. It is now twenty-seven minutes past eight. You may go into executive session at half-past eight, and at half-past nine I shall be ready to escort you either to your board-room at the office of the United Mints of North America, or to the dark but wholly secure safe-deposit vaults that I have designed for your accommodation in the subterranean suburbs of this little burg."

With these words, Aladdin departed.

At noon that day Monsieur Le Duc di

Lumière, with his mother the Countess de Bougie, and suite, arrived at the St. Gotham Hotel.

"There is a telegram for your Grace," observed the proprietor, as he entered the royal salon. He handed over the little yellow envelope. Aladdin tore it open hastily and read:

M. LE DUC DI LUMIÈRE, *Hotel St. Gotham:*
The Board of Directors of the United Mints of North America have secured control of sixty blocks in the heart of the tenement district of New York and will begin at once the erection of thirty first-class model tenement houses, costing two million apiece, each building fronting on all four sides upon a complete city square to be devoted to public parks for the people and playgrounds for the children. Can you supply janitors? Answer, collect.

(Signed) SILAS REDDYMUN,
JOHN W. MIDAS,
RUFUS BONDIFELLER.

A year later, while Aladdin and Mr. Bondifeller were returning from the opening ceremonies of the wonderful new tenements of lower New York in the latter's motor, the aged financier gave his young friend's hand a quick and affectionate pressure.

"Duke," said he, his voice trembling with happiness, "you have made me the happiest man in the world. When I looked out upon the sea of faces of those tenants of our new houses, as you made your address, and saw the look of hope in eyes that a year ago were filled with threatening and despair, it gave me such a thrill as I never had before. Is there anything else you can suggest wherein a man can use a few more millions for the benefit of humanity?"

"Yes," said Aladdin. "Now that you have done something for the poor, a few millions spent for the amelioration of the habits of the rich would be a great boon."

"And how would you go about it?" asked the old man.

"I don't know, Major," replied Aladdin. "It is a much harder proposition than the other."

"And meanwhile," said the old man, tremulously, "how can I show my own gratitude to you personally for all you have done for me?"

Aladdin looked across the car at the fair face of Marjorie Bondifeller, whose lovely eyes fell as they caught his glance.

"Well," said Aladdin, blushing a rosy red, "you might make me your son."

"Ah, my boy," sighed the Major, as he shook his head sadly, "I am afraid that is impossible. I don't think your mother would marry a cross-grained old curmudgeon like me. I've been a widower for so many years now that I have become set in my ways, and—"

"But there's another way round, ain't there?" cried Aladdin.

And there was, and that is how, my dear children, Marjorie Bondifeller happened to become the Duchess di Lumière.

THE END

Reprint Publishing

FOR PEOPLE WHO GO FOR ORIGINALS.

This book is a facsimile reprint of the original edition. The term refers to the facsimile with an original in size and design exactly matching simulation as photographic or scanned reproduction.

Facsimile editions offer us the chance to join in the library of historical, cultural and scientific history of mankind, and to rediscover.

The books of the facsimile edition may have marks, notations and other marginalia and pages with errors contained in the original volume. These traces of the past refers to the historical journey that has covered the book.

ISBN 978-3-95940-048-0

Facsimile reprint of the original edition
Copyright © 2015 Reprint Publishing
All rights reserved.

www.reprintpublishing.com

www.ingramcontent.com/pod-product-compliance
Lightning Source LLC
Chambersburg PA
CBHW051638260626
47170CB00004B/1223